→ For Pat
a souvenir
from home
while you're
in Costa Rica
With Love,
   Bruce
(a.k.a. Joel Redon)
   2-8-89
   N.Y.C.

Bloodstream
Joel Redon

 Knights
Press

Stamford, Connecticut

Wood cut for cover designed by J.M. Skowron
Cover designed by Chris Karukas

Published by Knights Press, P.O. Box 454, Pound Ridge, NY 10576
Distributed by Lyle Stuart, Inc.

Library of Congress Cataloging-in-Publication Data

Redon, Joel
    Bloodstream / by Joel Redon.
        p. cm.
    ISBN 0-915175-35-5 : $9.00
    I. Title.
    PS3568.E36424B5 1989
    813'.54—dc19   88-29256
                                                CIP

Printed in the United States of America

For V'Anne Didzun

It was like Sleeping Beauty magic...there would be the hundred years' sleep. I knew it in spite of the pain. The pain did not abate at all. It was still there, eating me up; but in the hundred years' sleep it would die. It couldn't live for a hundred years. And brambles would grow and everything turn marble-grey. The dust would be as thick and as exquisite to the touch as mole-skin; and there would be moonlight always.

— Denton Welch, *A Voice Through A Cloud*

Bloodstream

1

He took the side path, over the bridge where several of the gleaming red fish scurried underneath in the pale green water of a pool. It was murky and there were lily pads floating on it. He was surprised that the fish were for the most part still alive, left over from his twenty-fifth birthday party when all the ponds on the entire estate had been filled with fish, all kept from spilling out into the lake by tiny black screens. But most of them, purchased for the party from a tropical pet shop a month ago, were finally beginning to die.

He came out of the small forest and up the walk to the Tea House. Taking a seat on one of the deck chairs, he stared out at the inlet on the island where pounds and pounds of sand had been dumped to resemble a beach. That's where the boat had come in to take his birthday guests on rides across the lake. He hadn't gone on any of these tours. Next year he wouldn't even have a party.

Just then Peter spotted his sister Sara with her inevitable pruning shears coming down the path from the lookout point where their father had assembled a large stone seat.

"Hi," she called, somewhat reluctantly.

He pulled his mouth into a grin.

"Why don't you take that jacket off?" she asked. "It's warm."

But Peter was thinking: If that small red bubble near my eye is what I think it is, it is much too close to the eye itself to be operated on. I was dreading that this would happen to my face.

Disease: You can touch anything, don't touch my face.

Sara stood at the bottom of the trail looking at him.

A long dark train seemed to be speeding through Peter's head. He looked up at the hard sky. It was difficult enough accepting these tumors or lesions or whatever they were called on his arms and legs, but now. . . . Bravely, he smiled again, and began walking slowly back to the caretaker's cottage, which he used at present, and which looked something like an enormous gray Japanese pagoda from the outside. His sister lived in the basement of his parent's house, up above on the cliff. She did not know that he had AIDS.

There is nothing to do but ignore this lesion and go on, he told himself. He looked way up the hill at his parent's house on the Point and then crossed his private yard. Opening the Japanese screen and entering, he poked his finger playfully in the thin, almost transparent rice paper, making a hole as he had done when he was a kid — just for old times' sake. He made his way over to the black and red lacquer bar. There he took out a fifth of Dewars and poured some in a glass. He removed two ice cubes from the icebox, and dropped them in the glass; they sounded like pitch exploding in a fire. Settling back in an oval-backed wicker chair he stared out at the blue lake — at all of the boats and the people skiing or being towed on rubber tires. Then he looked up at the huge lesions he'd drawn on the wall that he occasionally threw darts at. They were modeled after the ones in a *National Geographic* article. Then, on second thought, he reached over and poured out his drink.

He picked up the newspaper, flipped through it, and read in an editorial: "Health is not just a matter of ridding the body of disease. Rather, it reflects the extent to which we have achieved a balance among our emotional states of mind, our life-styles, and the environments in which we live and work."

He opened his medicine chest filled with vitamins. Since there is no cure for AIDS, the only thing the doctor could tell him was to eat right, avoid stress, and, of course, take absolutely no drugs. His own body told him not to drink alcohol — it gave him herpes. So instead he dreamed about his old ways — drinking again, staying up all night. All it took was one lesion on his face to insure that he would not go running into town anymore and get lost for a week. Now it was vanity that was keeping him in check.

Every time he'd left a place or made some change in his life, there was always some person he'd seen briefly, met and whom he did not get to know well. When he remembered the person or any of the other people, it always hurt — whether he was remembering something good or something bad. Why did it always hurt? He was trying not to think about people. He was trying not to think about the years he'd spent in New York, a place he loved, but a fast, destructive city.

He remembered once thinking: How is it that I look handsome one day and not the next? Is it that I just think I'm handsome, or do I actually change?

Beautiful bodies, he went on thinking, should not grow old or live obscured in the country, in tiny towns. They should live in big cities where they can be seen.

That's stupid, he thought, what was I thinking that for?

It was strange to consider it, but he knew it was true that he was probably the only person in his entire hometown who had AIDS. This was a fact that his parents knew enough to keep secret. He didn't want his home burned to the ground; he didn't want any Fundamentalists coming around making his life any harder than it was. The important thing was not to lose his head and show people that he did not seriously want to live. But he knew that even if a vaccine could be found, a cure was doubtful. Once a person was infected, the scientists predicted, it was for life. He'd lost faith in religion a long time ago; was it time to lose faith in modern science?

The passion he used to have for life was gone, that was certain. Everything seemed stupid now. Getting drunk didn't make a difference. Because of all he'd been through since his diagnosis, he had made his friends older, just as he had made himself. Was he defeated by having AIDS? Would he wage a war against the disease and lose? How would he even know if he'd won that war?

Deterioration.

He guessed it made sense, Didn't he push it to the limit? Not many people pushed it as far as he had and survived. He wasn't strong enough. It wasn't that he'd accidentally slept with the wrong person; AIDS had come, as it had for most, through repeated exposure. It came as a result of pushing week after week, year after year. He was tired. Washed up at twenty-five? He laughed at this. But he hadn't thought it would come out this way at all. How did he think it would have been? He had never looked ahead. "Having AIDS," someone had written in a book on the subject, "was not beautiful; it was painful, miserable, and depressing. It was like being told you were going to die in a car accident at some point in the next year. Nobody told where or when you were going to die, just that you would perish."

Two Vitamin C pills, three Vitamin E's — for the skin —. and one garlic tablet to insure against a cold. He swallowed them down.

Ordinary things had never given him much pleasure. This had always been true. He had his own apartment once in New York on the Lower East Side, and its emptiness gave him a sick feeling. It was a nice apartment. But after that, for five years, he lived with other people, or in hotels paid for by the week, as people do during times of war. He was living during a war, that was for certain, a war that he didn't expect to see end. It would take a lot of courage, he knew, from now on, to see this thing through. He didn't like what was happening. It was hard to escape a sense of punishment. A lover had once warned him, "If you play, you pay." What a stupid simplistic thing to say! he'd thought then. But now he could see that it rather made sense. He wondered if that lover was still alive. He didn't know. He carried around too many deaths as it was; they were wounds, and he had roughly six of them. Letters were coming all the time.

He turned on the television and watched it until he fell asleep. When his mother had brought lunch down to him, he woke up long enough to eat it. His body ached and he closed his eyes afterwards.

Nature, like the ocean, is God itself, he thought later that afternoon as he pushed the motorboat out with his feet from the boathouse. Then, at the last possible moment, he jumped in and started the engine. It was no longer cool out and would not be until sunset. On the lake it was only cool during the day, before noon. He never liked the heat. As far as he was concerned, rain was the best weather. He often sat in the Tea House and watched during those times.

The lake was choppy and the front of the boat came down hard each time it slapped against a wave. He continued heading for the Canals, which in fact were no longer very beautiful. The number of houses on the lake had tripled. He could thank people like his father for that. There was nothing to look at anymore but houses, and since his father was in real estate that's all Peter ever heard about – prices, which ones were on the market, which firm had the most listings, what happened at the title company, the multiple listing service. "Houses are a very big part of life, just like food. You can't get away from real estate," his father would say.

When he got back to the dock he could see Sara leaning against the boathouse, smoking. He slowed down so he wouldn't spray her with water as he pulled in.

"Do you want a ride?" he called politely.

She threw down her cigarette sullenly. "All right," she said. She hopped into the boat. He shifted gears and aimed the bow

back out to the center of the lake. He looked at her occasionally and noted how well she was — still time to make mistakes.

"Do you like it out here?" she asked.

"Sure," he said.

Looking at her skin, at how healthy it was, he felt
poisoned, like a food product gone sour.

"Are you going to New York this winter?" she asked,
making conversation.

"I'm staying here," he answered.

It was obvious that there must be a reason. She looked
surprised, but let it pass.

"We'll have to think of things to do together," he said,
trying not to sound forced.

Sara, like Peter, was a quiet, private person, only more
so. They were both ice cubes, in fact, that needed a little
melting, and they understood this about each other. But
Peter was miles ahead of his sister; he could talk much more
openly to people than she could. He used to go out of his way
to talk to her, but now he avoided her. He felt comfortable
enough with her, but at this point in the game he did not want
to force intimacies any further on her than he had before.

Now that the fog around the lake had cleared and the
late afternoon sun had come out, he felt empty inside. He
pushed the boat up to sixty miles per hour.

"Is there something bothering you?" she asked.

"No," he answered sharply, and his once chance to tell
her that he had AIDS was gone.

When he woke the sun was setting. The sky was purple like
the lesions on his body. Then it was even darker.

Pain doesn't amount to anything, he was thinking as he
lay in darkness listening to the crickets outside. He could cry
all night and it meant little. Tears couldn't change his world.
They were only wasted. They came suddenly, unexpectedly.

They came when he was staring at a blank wall. They gathered up in his eyes and he would try to blink them away. He knew he looked all right, but for how much longer? He didn't want ever to have to deal with people's arrogance toward the sick, their lack of compassion. This troubled him. "Sweep away the corpses," he could imagine people saying to each other, "there are new people standing in line."

Wouldn't it be better, after all, to die right now than to live through the agony of waiting?

It seemed as though he hadn't slept for months. He wanted to go to sleep. Did that mean that he accepted his death? It would be nice . . . to lie down in a hot bath, the water up to his chin, to fall asleep. But there was no sleep.

People must see it in my face, he thought. Sara can see that I'm not the same. Should I be ashamed? Thank God it's not painless, that's all I can say. If it was painless it would be much worse. This way I can say that when I do die I won't hurt anymore. He wished he could put off worrying about if for another year, like paying up a landlord so he wouldn't have to worry about rent. It was remarkable how similar the feelings were — not having money for food and wondering if you were shortly going to die. But, of course, it wasn't really the same.

2

The best thing about mornings on the lake, Peter thought, was the air. The lake was still, there isn't a sound or a single movement, everything is gray and clear. Dusk was similar to morning, only warmer, the same pale blues and greens except that the sun was an unusual bright neon orange.

Peter stretched and looked out the sliding glass doors and saw his father mowing the lawn. This meant that his father had been drinking and felt guilty, or wanted Peter and his mother to feel guilty for excluding him from their present conversation. Peter and his mother were sitting together on the flower-print couch finishing breakfast.

Peter's mother had been a very beautiful woman; he remembered her being so. He'd never been embarrassed as an adolescent when his schoolmates saw them together, at a play, a gallery, at the supermarket — not embarrassed as he'd been with his father whom he was ashamed of (but not because he wasn't goodlooking). It was sad that his mother had shrunk. Her face had gone soft. This had all happened in five to seven years, the length of time he'd been away. He wondered if he'd been responsible for the loss of her beauty.

"I like my children to be adults," his mother was saying that morning. "I don't want to be a disciplinarian anymore."

"Do you wish I'd gotten married and had kids?"

This was the kind of conversation they often had, late at night, when his father was in bed, waiting impatiently, jealously, for his wife to join him, to stop talking forever to Peter, It had always been that way.

"Sometimes I think it would have been nice to have kids," Peter said.

"I know," she said smiling, "so you could raise them better than we raised you. I had the same notions. We all did. Do you know, I can never talk like this with anyone?"

﹒ Both Peter and his mother agreed that his grandmother's death was one of the worst things that had ever happened to them both, but the night of Peter's diagnosis was actually worse because Peter was in New York and had to telephone the news.

"I wasn't with you," she said, "and when your grandma died all I remembr is cuddling with you all night.

"Your father doesn't discuss his feelings," she went on. "He bottles it all up inside. He doesn't have any friends." *He has me!*

Spread out on the table was an enormous file of newspaper clippings. His mother had been collecting them and putting them in a drawer along with her knitting patterns and cooking recipes. He picked up one of the clippings and read: "Researchers say people who rid themselves of emotional burdens by telling others about personal woes strengthen their immune systems and are less likely to fall ill."

"I just want you to be happy," she said finally.

"There's something I always wanted to ask you," he said, starting on a new subject. "I mean, this is from a long time ago. Did Grandma ever talk to you about something. . .?" He was having a difficult time putting it into words. "I was thinking about her last night and about what a good disciplinarian she was. I mean, once she told me to be careful and I broke something. When she scolded me I went into the guest bedroom and she came in and asked for *my* forgiveness. She asked me to please not be mad at *her.* I never forgot that."

"My mother was not a disciplinarian," she explained. "She hated to have people mad at her."

"But, anyway. You know how Dad used to sort of abuse me?"

His mother gave him a particular look.

"Well, once I talked to Grandma about it and I told her I didn't think you were doing enough to stop it, and I asked grandma if she'd talk to you. Did she ever?" He didn't think she could remember back to that particular conversation that had occurred perhaps thirteen years before. But she did.

"She asked me once if your father mistreated you, but she didn't say that you'd said anything."

A fragment from his childhood reading suddenly rushed back to him: "At my grandmother's house there are two tall trees on each side of the road. They close up their branches at the top. When I go underneath I shut up my coat because I always think it's colder there."

In a sense, what he'd begun to realize was that by coming home to live on the lake he was coming back to his mother. Whenever he got too put out with the world he came home to her, as he had done now. His mother was his friend; they could sit in the sun together and talk, walk in the garden, go to the water. At these moments thay were inseparable, no one could come between them – Sara, Peter's friends, his sexuality, her husband. If he was going to die soon, he wanted to be with her; he didn't want his friends from New York or Los Angeles. He didn't want his father. His mother was a reasonable woman. They used to exchange books; he would check out three from the library and so would she; later they traded. Since coming back to his parents, he liked to read, at least when he felt well enough.

He took out his old set of F. Scott Fitzgerald novels that she'd given him one Christmas. When he read them as a kid none of the plots resembled what he now understood. Yet he couldn't get the old visual impressions out of his mind. Today she was reading Mishima now and Peter, who knew of Mishima's homosexual themes, was delighted. She found these books serene and poetic. He did, too, but she admitted that she really liked Kawabata more. He thought it was amusing, earlier, when he'd flipped through the pages of the Mishima novel and found one sentence that he underlined in pencil when she'd left the room: "He was coming to the inescapable conclusion that society is governed by the rule of heterosexuality, that endlessly tiresome principle of majority rule." He though that Mishima was the perfect representative of his world, to educate his mother on the subject. Mishima was individual but universal at the same time.

Unlike his mother, Peter's father had a problem with communication, as did most men. Feelings were taboo. Peter had seen that the marriages of most all of his parents' friends had ended in divorce because of extramarital affairs. Peter asked his mother if all men cheated on their wives. She said she thought that they did.

"Does it embarass Dad that I have AIDS?" he suddenly asked. "Would it, I mean, if people found out?"

"I don't know what he feels," she answered. "I have never been able to tell."

"You know what the essence of my childhood is?" He was looking out at the lake. "It's you reading to me from those set of books, *ChildCraft,* and that poem, the Pirate Don Durk of Dundee."

Her eyes lit up. "But that's the essence of my childhood, too!" She said, excited, "Your grandmother read me those poems. How funny. I could never forget the rhythms: 'It's true he was wicked as wicked could be, his sins they out numbered a hundred and three, but oh, he was perfectly gorgeous to see, the Pirate Don Durk of Dundee.' " She looked at Peter. "It's nice having breakfast with you," she said. "I'm very glad you're home. And now," she told him quietly, "I don't feel so swallowed up by your father. We've been alone without kids for some years. He certainly is annoyed now when you and I talk."

Talking. It was so much better now than back in the days of frustrated adolescence when he was unable to translate into words what he thought and felt.

After breakfast, when Peter said goodbye and went down to the caretaker's cottage at the bottom of the hill, he sat near the swimming pool below and ate some raspberries that were warm and soft from the sun.

"The people who think they're going to live usually do, and the others don't." These words of wisdom from a social worker had given Peter great hope whenever he recalled them. All I have to do is believe that I will live, he thought. Yes. But I can believe that only as long as I'm not in pain.

He could see Sara across the way, looking out at the lake pensively, smoking a cigarette. He remembered once she'd told him: "I could never look my high school teachers in the eye." He thought that probably meant something significant about her.

3

When Peter was younger he remembered a school chum telling him that all people had a double, that somewhere in the world there was another person who looked just like you. He thought about this, but it wasn't as important to him as his own personal notion that all people were really just part of a conspiracy, that he was the only person in the world, and that his fate was arranged by all those others around him. His mother, his sister, everyone could read his mind, see through the walls to his bedroom where he lay. He was certain that they were always trying to trap him, to test his emotional endurance. They were not human — he was the only real h uman. As an adult, he felt that groups of people, especially strangers, were his enemies. He must protect himself. He tried to compose his face like a mask, but people could see that he was doing this and so they knew he was nervous and guarding himself. Nothing worked. His lips gave away more about him than his eyes.

When he came in the first time to this AIDS Support Group, at the home of a social worker, Peter was aware of the members turning their faces; he was uneasy and he knew they saw this. He hoped that as he got used to each of the faces, no new people would come so that he would have to start all over again.

When the meeting had begun, each person introduced himself and said what was on his mind, what his conflicts had been for the week. When it was Peter's turn he sat up in his chair and scratched his arm. He crossed his legs and cleared his throat. He was the last one to speak.

"AIDS is not an immediate death sentence," the social worker started to tell the group after Peter's brief and, he thought, innocuous speech. The social worker had already introduced himself and given an account of his thoughts regarding the week. "Contrary to what the media tells us," he went on, "there are some drugs that can prolong our lives; and it is very important that we believe in positive thinking.

Ha! Peter thought, that's what you think. You don't have AIDS. All you care about is finding yourself a lover. A lover is just a barrier between you and life; you're only bored.

The next man to speak was black; he spoke of his experience with prejudice – of his being black, gay, and a person with AIDS – all three. He was a warm person, Peter decided. The man said, "If I gave in to society I'd be dead by now. I learned not to let things stop me. I had to."

Another man in the group had been recently fired from his job in a gay bar because he had AIDS. At this first meeting Peter attended he was outraged: Where was this man's political responsibility? He had been dismissed for having AIDS and had done nothing about it! Peter delicately suggested that the man owed it to the gay community to expose this bit of hypocrisy within its ranks. The social worker intervened, "Decisions of this nature are up to the individual," Peter kept quiet after that.

Another man had a harried look. Peter pegged him for an intellectual. He seemed a little out of control, with glasses he kept pushing up on his nose. His name was Yale; Peter thought that was a little odd.

He trained his eyes on a Don Bachardy pencil drawing above the social worker's head. The group met in the social worker's home. There were new AIDS therapy pamphlets on the dining table – information, among other things, about hydrogen peroxide to bathe in. In the kitchen they had coffee, non-decaffeinated, and fruit juices. Smoking wasn't allowed.

Peter was nervous. He didn't like the practice of ending the meeting by hugging each member. He didn't like the small talk during the breaks – everything was upsetting to him. He was uncomfortable with himself. Mostly he was tired; with it came bewilderment.

Initially, since the date of Peter's diagnosis he had little interest in meeting new people. He did not want to talk with people who had AIDS, either. But not that he was doing so, after he realized his mother and his friends could not completely understand his emotional predicament, he was glad. At this point he even preferred these people to his old friends. He found little comfort in a remark like this: "My gums started to give out last week (as Peter's had): I think I might have a lesion on my arm, but I'm not sure that's what it is. My doctor wants to put me on AZT but I'm afraid to do it – it makes me feel like I'm lying down to die if I start to take medication."

"What you're experiencing right now is denial." the social worker said. "But you can't afford to put off taking AZT, which has a strong tendency to lessen the symptoms and prolong life."

Denial. It struck a chord in Peter. That's why I was drinking so heavily this summer, he thought. I couldn't face the fact that I had AIDS. I didn't want to accept the responsibility I had toward myself – so I drank and it made my condition worse. Six months. That's how much longer I would have lasted, and it would have been awful and not just for me, but for everyone concerned – in and out of the hospital. I was denying to myself that I had AIDS. I was trying to forget.

Suddenly he understood that he'd been in a state of denial and that was the reason he didn't stop drinking when he knew he should have and why he'd continued to use cocaine. So now it was a question not of what he was doing for his health but what he was doing not to jeopardize it. The next step was spiritual. There was no getting around the word, as much as he hated its overtones. He needed once more to hear the instructor tell him, "People who believe they're going to live are generally the ones who do; the people who believe they won't live are usually the ones who don't." That was the key and Peter knew it. He had his work cut out for him.

As to medication and the fact that Peter, like the man who'd spoken, was not taking any — Peter's reasons were more complicated — at this point it had nothing to do with denial. Other than feeling like a shut-in, what was he doing for his health? AZT, the only drug available to help prevent the onset of the illness (if it even worked), Peter was at this point ineligible for: his T-cell count was a little too high. It seemed as if doctors were saying to him: "There's nothing we can do for you, we can't control these infections (routinely he had highly irritated rashes, from head to foot; it was common), just go home and die. Figure it out for yourself." And that's what he was trying to do with his vitamin regimen. At the moment it was the only thing he could think of to do for himself.

The young man went on speaking, "I didn't have a very good self-image. I abused myself and then for two years I've been clean and now suddenly I get this."

The worst thing about drying out, Peter reflected, is that you get so puritanical. How can I judge this guy or anyone else? Life is far too complicated. God, the things I've done myself — it's amazing, difficult even to digest. Passion was always sordid.

He looked at the young man again. But he looks so healthy, he thought, and then: That's what people tell me, too, but if they only knew what it takes just to maintain a healthy look that passes for normal!

He darted a glance about the room at the five people in it. He smiled. He wondered if he was the only one looking around and trying to decide what symptoms each person had. By looking you couldn't always tell if a person had AIDS. But under their shirts were there large purple splotches? Did they have night sweats? Horrible rashes? For the most part everyone looked just a little dissipated, but no different from the ordinary people you encountered in bars, on Castro Street, on Second Avenue, Santa Monica Boulevard, on the subway.

"What's the most depressing is the media," one of them was saying. "They make it look as if we're all going to die, that there's no hope. Well, there *is.*"

It's amazing, Peter thought, that four little spots on my body should catapult me into such a depression, just four little marks. . . .

"On the other hand," the group leader pointed out, "we need the media to alert people to the point where they'll do something about it. You have to hit them to get them to move. And the government is not going to do anything until people force them to. It's always been this way. Don't watch those television programs that tell people that AIDS patients are all going to die."

But we can't help it, Peter thought; we need to feel that in some ways we understand what's happening to us. How can you tell people not to watch television? We don't want to feel alone.

For the rest of the meeting people discussed food, places they'd been, and indulged in general small talk. Peter yawned and contributed nothing. The meeting had become a strain; he was tired. He also knew that his father would be waiting outside with the car. Peter used to cringe when he was a boy and his father picked him up from school in a Cadillac Fleetwood or a Rolls-Royce Phantom V. It was humiliating. None of the other kids were ever picked up by their parents in such cars. Regular people drove regular cars. Now he had no thoughts on the matter. Exhausted, he was just glad there was any car at all.

It is ridiculous being this tired, he thought. He'd only gotten out of bed three hours before. He wondered if it was a phase. He hoped so. It couldn't get worse than this, not if he took care of himself. But that was just it; how could he take any better care? Stop it, he thought, stop thinking, just stop thinking. . . . But it was like trying to stop a despised tune from playing over and over in one's head. He wondered what the psychological explanation was for these obsessions, for not being able to control one's thinking. When he was little he used to picture objects in his mind, but something would always happen to them; whether it was a plane or himself, a destructive force would come into contact with the object. No matter how hard he tried to control it otherwise, he could never get the plane to a safe landing. In fact, the more he tried the more impossible it became. He had a recurring image of his finger being caught in a car door and snapping off at the end.

His father. . . It was not certain to Peter whether his Dad was his ally or his enemy, nor whether the two of them were in mortal competition or not. Over what? Peter's mother.

But why compete at all? Hadn't his father remarked often enough: "Women have been telling me what to do all my life – my mother, your mother. I don't ever want to work for a woman. I don't need them."

Peter's father was a dour alcoholic and never contradicted his German mother who was ninety and typed books in braille for blind students. She aways referred to Peter as "Peterchen." Peter didn't like any of that side of his family. It was too filled with manipulation over family money – one side getting all, people being left out of wills because of prejudices. They were hard people, untrusting and severe; they were white supremacists, bigots. They are inflicted with the sickness of capitalism, Peter thought, an acute state of selfishness. His father was reading a biography of J. Paul Getty and there were always several World War Two spy thrillers about the house –

men in positions of supreme power. His father had a habit of waving from his car to every policeman or city official; they never saw him or paid attention, and wondered what he was waving at. Joking, storekeepers addressed him as "Mayor."

But as far as money itself was concerned Peter wouldn't hesitate to say that his father was generous with it — "sloppy," his mother would say.

"So how did your meeting go?"

Peter slid into the seat next to his father. The air conditioning was on high and the stale flat Muzak background common to elevators was playing. His father was smoking a cigar.

"It went all right." Peter didn't even bother to say that people had talked about their feelings, feelings being something his father didn't understand.

When they got home Peter slept all afternoon and had dinner sent down. For the first time in several days he resorted to television. He watched the music videos and only paid particular attention when they had nothing to do with sex. Sex was too simple.

As he watched he could feel a bump on the side of his tongue. He rubbed it against his teeth. At a commercial break he went into the bathroom and looked in the mirror. There he saw an enormous white area protruding along the edge of his tongue. His hands went up, his face contorted. He looked again and felt sick.

An hour later his father came down to inspect the boathouse and make sure everything was locked up for the night, and to pick up Peter's dinner tray. He saw that Peter was upset and asked him why. Peter showed him his tongue.

"Isn't there something you can take for that?" he asked, casually.

"There is nothing I can take," Peter said, impatiently, his anger building. "What you've got to understand is that there is no medication. That's why people who have AIDS die."

"Well," his father said, heading for the door, "we'll look at it tomorrow. It looks like a cold sore to me. Can't you put some medication on it?"

Peter looked hard at his father, "It's not a cold sore," he said firmly.

"Well, can't you put cold-sore medication on it just to see?"

"What do you think?" Peter snapped. "It's internal, not external. And how long do you think ointment would last in your mouth anyway?" He had a difficult time accepting that his father could be so stupid. It disgusted him.

"I don't know what you were talking to your mother about the other night but she was in tears later and didn't sleep." With that parting shot, Peter's father left.

Peter watched him go. Once he'd calmed down he drafted a letter to his father:

"Dear Dad, please don't be disturbed if you see Mom crying. I like to think that emotions are good things and that if she cries it is healthy. I know you are concerned that I might be making it hard on her, but the truth is that the very fact that we are discussing things makes it easier for me. I need emotional support. Her tears are a small price to pay. I need people I can talk to. So, this is to say that if you hear any moans or groans don't be upset; it's probably only natural and it's probably not bad. Thanks for your understanding. Your son."

Imagine me having to write this letter to anybody! he thought. To apologize for emotions. . . .

When at last he slept, Peter dreamed that he was in a coffee shop where he was talking to an old friend with whom he had once been romantically interested. During the conversation it occured to Peter that he hadn't told the friend he had AIDS. When he did, the friend changed the subject and wanted to leave the restaurant. When Peter suggested somewhere else, his friend wasn't in the mood. "I'm not interested in trying to seduce you anymore." Peter lost his temper. "Shut up!" he said. The friend was not affected. Peter, wearing an enormous sweater, was trying to push his hands out through the cuffs. He had mittens on, too, which made it all the more difficult. Two girls were now sitting at the table and he realized they were watching him. As his struggle grew more and more futile, the girls laughed at him. He tried to take the sweater off but stopped, remembering that there were embarassing lesions on his body. His friend was gone. Peter had the vague impression later that his dream had been about sexual rejection.

4

In the morning Peter opened the window to let some of the moisture evaporate from the bathroom mirror. His face came into focus. He could see tiny lesions beginning to form under his eye and on his forehead. There were also suspicious growths that could — or could not — be acne above his lip and to the side of his nose. But he couldn't tell for certain. He could only wait to see what would happen. Somehow he had to escape the feeling of waiting, because if he was waiting, what was he waiting for, except to die?

He dried himself off with a towel and closed the shower door. Then he turned back to the mirror.

The government's administration didn't seem overly concerned with the plight of people like Peter who had AIDS. Scientists were doing all they could; but there was very little anyone could do for him. There was reason for despair, but you can only despair for so long and then it becomes difficult to continue. The world of despair has no boundary, yet it is finite.

So what do you do? You take a shower every morning, you shave, you brush your teeth, you swallow a handful of vitamins, you dress nicely, and you eat a big breakfast. Then, he thought, you take it from there.

Ambition used to be an important word; part of that word's application had to do with New York. You did not tend to be ambitious when living at home with your parents – that was "retirement." But was he ready to retire? Of course not. Yet you needed ambition to conjure up a force of will; frankly, Peter didn't know if he had it. Would it be wise to fly off to New York and start over? Wouldn't the strain be too much? Wouldn't he end up pushing himself too far again, staying up all night, not eating enough? His friends had told him, "Stay at home at least until you've learned how to live without nightclubs and drinking, then come back and live here once your new lifestyle has been firmly established. Just remember, when you think you're losing your footing, that you haven't gone home to die."

He washed out his disposable shaver, put his toothbrush away and ran his fingers through his hair. Then he opened the door and a gush of steam followed him out. As he started to climb the stairs the phone rang.

"There's someone here to see you," It was Sara's voice, troubled, calling to him. "He says he's from your AIDS group."

Peter's face suddenly felt hot. This was so unexpected he didn't give himself time to think. He hurried up to his parent's house, distressed that Sara had found out the truth.

At the top of the trail the dogs were barking. He wished they'd stop. He flailed his arms, but that only made them bark louder. When he climbed the stairs to the deck he could see Sara facing him through the large windows, with a repressed but terrified look. His mother was speaking to a young man with glasses and fanatical green eyes. Peter recognized Yale from his AIDS groups. Now, what's this all about? he thought apprehensively. The young man was dressed shabbily, as Peter remembered him from before, and he too looked tired.

Peter's mother and the young man stood with cups of coffee in their hands. As Peter opened the sliding glass doors and entered, he subdued his anxiety.

"Hello." Peter nodded his head. "How are you?"

They shook hands and Peter turned inquisitively towards his mother for an explanation.

"Yale doesn't live very far from here," she said cheerfully. "Why don't the two of you sit out on the porch and
I'll bring you more coffee?"

It wasn't that Peter was misanthropic. He did like
people, but he didn't know what to talk about. For him there
was only one thing, and he was not even certain that other
people faced with this problem wanted to talk about it.

Sometimes he played a game in his mind where for five
minutes he knew how long he would live. He would only be
allowed to write down his reaction, *fair,* or *unfair,* on a piece
of paper. Then when the five minutes were over, he would
no longer know. He would only have left the slip of paper
with the word *fair* or *unfair* written on it. He thought that
if he wrote *unfair* down then he would know that he had
a very short life ahead and he would therefore begin immediately to accept this fact; otherwise, if it said *fair,* he would
have nothing to worry about for now. But this was not the
case, and so there was nothing else to think about. But he
couldn't be sure if others who had AIDS felt this way.

Peter let Yale speak first. It wasn't hospitable, but Peter
could only do what he was able to.

"I don't really live nearby," Yale apologized. "I just said
that." He sat out on the porch swing and put his feet gingerly
on the rail, staring out over the bank to the tip of the island
where Peter's cottage was. He looked out at the lake dotted
with tiny blobs of buoys bobbing up and down. Even though
it was a warm day, there were very few boats out.

"So where do you live?" Peter inquired. He was sitting
on one of the ice-cream-parlor chairs. He crossed his legs and
recklessly took a cigarette from one of his father's East Indian
boxes that were all over the house. He would feel dehydrated
after smoking, and his eyes might hurt, but he *had* to have one.

"I live in the city," Yale said.

"How do you make your money?" Peter asked.

"I sell used books to bookstores. I'm a book scout. I buy

them at estates and garage sales. I'm always looking at the classifieds. But I'm on Social Security now and I have Medicare, to pay for most of my hospital bills."

"What nationality?" It was a ridiculous habit, asking people this, but Peter had picked it up in New York where practically everyone was strictly Italian, German, Irish, Jewish, Brazilian, you name it. The only people he didn't ask were WASPS or blacks.

"Jewish," Yale answered.

Peter was surprised. This for all intents and purposes was good news; he always liked Jewish people in particular — why he couldn't say, but they'd always been good friends in New York. "That's because there's so many of us," one of his friends, Avi, had said; "You can't help it." But that was only partly it. Jews had a sense of the absurd, of pathos – the combination of humor and tragedy. They also like to try out their ideas.

"I got your address from the social worker," Yale said, not taken aback by Peter's question.

Peter's eyes widened; he was intrigued.

"I mean," Yale said, gulping down his coffee, "our group leader didn't give it to me, I looked on his attendance page." He fingered the hole in the knee of his jeans. "So how have you been since Friday?"

"I'm okay," Peter said optimistically. Then, with more determination, "I think I'm okay."

"Would you like to come over to my house and play cards?"

Peter would have laughed or thought Yale was crazy a year ago, but things were different now. People were different. He saw delicacy and fragility, and he saw it in himself, in everything. Laughing at anyone was stupid.

"Yeah," he replied, "I'd like to do that."

Yale put down his cup. "You have a lot of property," he said.

"My father's in real estate," Peter answered by way of

apology. "Would you like to go down to the lake?"
"Sure I would."

"Do you like living with your parents? The sunsets out here
must be remarkable, unreal."
"That's because of the clouds," Peter explained. "The sun
reflects the colors off of them."
"But you like living here?"
"It's boring," Peter said. "But I'd much rather be bored
than feel as if time was moving too quickly."
"True?"
"Sometimes I think it is."
Yale was driving swiftly along Macadam Avenue, heading
for Portland. Passing John's Landing they could see occasional
glimpses of the Willamette river between the warehouses.
"Are the bathhouses still open in Oregon?" Peter asked,
making light conversation and feeling pleasant, the breeze
against his cheek.
"Most cities in America still have them," Yale said. "The
government only closed the ones in large cities, the rest of
them just pay hush money and go on operating like they do
here. I've never been to this one."
Peter was a little surprised that Yale knew so much about
bathhouses; he didn't seem like the type, whatever that would
be.
"What I'm trying to figure out," Peter said as they came
up the ramp into Portland, and passed the old Chinese
restaurant that was made over into a Xerox shop, "is what
to do about AZT. They say my T-cell count is just over 200
and 200 is the cut off. One doctor advised me to go out and
drink for a week because it would bring my T-cell count down.
I'm serious. So what do I have to do to get it?"
"AZT," Yale said with authority, "is the great pacifier. They
give it to you and tell you to shut up. I don't know if it even

works. Most of the people I know got anemic and had to have blood transfusions, and after six months it gradually got more toxic. Then the white cells went. People got headaches, aggravation, restlessness, and insomnia. The long-term toxicity is still unknown. I think DTC may be better: you can get its effects by using antabuse, which after a few hours turns into the same properties. I mean, it has something in it called Imuthiol that raises T-cells." They passed under the Hawthorne Bridge. Yale pointed to a strip of green by the seawall. "This is a pretty park."

Peter didn't look. "What should I be doing then?" he asked.

"Interferon isn't bad, some people say. The side effects are about the same as you get with AZT – nausea, headaches, the shakes and chills. Some people say it's not as bad as AZT and that's probably true, but it's very expensive, more than AZT, and I'd be surprised if insurance would cover it. Besides, who can tell if there's really that much improvement with it anyway?"

"Isn't interferon what they give to sick cows?"

Yale gave him a glance.

"I read it somewhere," Peter said. "I also know you can get a darkroom solution and rub it on your lesions."

"That's called DNCB," Yale told him, "and you put the liquid on a part of your body once a week for a month to stimulate T-cells, but the lotion part that you put directly on the lesions every few days can make them open up if you use too much, and they can get infected. So you have to be careful with it. That's what I use on mine. Now, the other drug, AL-721 with lecithin, is the one people go to Israel for. They say it works good except the only way to get it here is to buy home-made stuff with mayonnaise and olive oil. That's not how they make it in Israel. It's not pure here. Lots of times it's contaminated with bacteria. We can't get federal approval for general use of AL-721 before 1989, if we get it even then.

So that's why we have these grass-roots underground drug movements, guerrilla clinics – like the one I go to. Who knows if AL-721 is good or bad for everyone, anyway. It's not the same stuff, we know that. At least that's what the doctors say. I don't know" He turned up onto the bridge going southeast.

"But who *does* know?" Peter asked.

"Your parents are rich, aren't they?" He smiled. "Why don't you have them send you to Germany and have your blood drained and put in some new stuff — like the rock stars do when they're strung out and don't want to go through withdrawals. Ozone therapy."

"Very funny," Peter said. He looked down at his hand. "Did you say you used DNCB? Do you have any?"

"I have some at home. That's partly why I came to see you. The other day you told the group you couldn't get AZT, and I was glad, because I don't think it's much of an answer. I want you to try this instead. We'll put some on you when we get to my place."

Peter nodded and they rode along in silence.

"Do you find yourself getting weird?" Peter asked finally, "I mean, now that you have AIDS?"

"What do you mean – weird?"

Peter squinted his eyes and looked down at the water under the bridge. He used to be afraid of bridges, and car accidents. . .high places. That hadn't changed. "Well, I keep having these flashes of things I used to believe, or just the strangest tidbits."

"Tidbits?"

"You've heard the word. You know, like just a minute ago I was thinking about trick-or-treating and when I saved up the very best Halloween candy and ate only choice selections every few days and what constituted a rare jewel in my collection and how long they lasted and why. Thoughts about the past."

"The important thing to remember here," Yale said,

joking, "is that you probably always had weird thoughts to begin with. But I know about these things because I read a lot."

"And I knew you were weird when I first saw you," Peter said.

"As I did you."

"That's great," Peter said sarcastically. "That's just great." But he thought to himself: When you are dying all you want is life. When you have life you want something more. Yet he couldn't say this suddenly outloud. He said nothing at all.

At the third stoplight they turned left.

"Let me see your lesions," Yale asked, once they were at his studio.

Peter pulled down his pants and pointed out the purple splotches.

"Not only does DNCB help fade these," Yale said, "but it also helps your system heal itself better in the future. Hold out your arm."

Peter watched him as Yale put on a spot of the medication and then bandaged it.

"I get this stuff from a guerrilla clinic that somebody has in his home near here. But even if you get this drug, you should also go on an antiviral like AL-721 or AZT."

"This is all too complicated to me," Peter said with exasperation. "How is anyone expected to know all this?"

"Because," Yale said quite seriously, "to have AIDS is also to have a new career. In order to heal yourself you have to go through a whole education, an uncharted one. It's one of the hardest educations there is, because as Christopher Isherwood says: 'If AIDS is God's will, then God's will must be circumvented.' This stuff takes work."

Something was happening inside Peter. He felt something close to gratitude. He was glad to have met Yale. He studied his features.

He could feel the liquid of the drug against his skin, and already he imagined the virus inside him that was eating away his cells, being assaulted dead in its tracks.

"I remember reading a long time ago," Peter said, "that you should be suspicious of suicide for people when they start giving all their things away. But I've always been like that, with few possessions. I wonder if that means instinctively I knew I was going to die."

"Ach, I doubt it, Peter," Yale said. He put a pencil in his mouth and chewed on it, making fresh, clean bites.

Yale lived in a studio that was very small. There was a peculiar wicker basket on the wall, a very bad oil painting of a desert with cactus life, and there were checkered window curtains. The walls were a brownish gray. Peter didn't know exactly what color it was. It annoyed him for awhile until it occured to him to ask.

"I don't know. Could it be army surplus color?"

"Beats me."

They sat on the bed. "I want to read you something," Yale said. "It has to do with an abstract theory of mine I've been working on in my diary. I'm wondering how much courage it takes to handle the fact that you're dying and how that makes you grow up crookedly but quickly. Then, just as you're going through all of these changes — these alterations of perceptions — you die. Is it worth it? Would I rather not learn what I have, and live to an old age, or get AIDS and learn a few things, minus the pain? Kierkegaard said people who are infinitely interested in themselves are drawn to sickness. And aren't gay men infinitely interested in themselves, anyway? And isn't AIDS the perfect narcissistic illness — a need to indulge oneself?"

"Yale," Peter spoke bluntly, the burning from the DNCB beginning to increase on the underside of his arm, "I don't know what you're talking about. Of course it's better not to have AIDS." Then at the same time he began thinking: Yale and I are very similar types. He wondered if Yale noticed it yet. Maybe Yale had noticed it even before Peter had. Something to do with sensibility. He looked up at the bookshelf, to see what sort of books Yale had. The first book that caught his eye was by Ernest Hemingway. He cringed as a young Englishman might when you tell him your favorite writer is Virginia Woolf. He'd assumed that Yale would have more esoteric tastes. He began chewing his lip. Then as he did so he noticed a bump inside his mouth. An old familiar momentary panic flashed through him. He tried not to show his distress and made up his mind to say nothing. He didn't want to upset anyone or spoil his day. But it isn't supposed to get worse, he thought. I'm supposed to get really sick and then, as in the movies just before the end, a cure will be found. It isn't supposed to happen that I really die. Besides, Peter would be letting down his daughter if he did . . .

When Peter had left home for the first time seven years ago, he imagined, much like George and Martha in the movie *Who's Afraid of Virginia Woolf,* that he was a father, and that he had an imaginary daughter who would grow up with him. Since Peter's first clear memories of people were roughly from age four, he knew that he would have to live his life more stably at certain points in order not to be a bad influence on his daughter. So if he had AIDS, that meant he had failed as a parent. Of course, he understood Martha's despair in *Virginia Woolf* when George announce that their imaginary son was dead. Peter empathized perfectly. His own daughter was dead, too: she had AIDS.

"Yale," Peter said, "I want you to know right now how nice I think you've been to me. You know I would have sat by that stupid lake with my parents and just let everything fall down on me, and maybe it still will — but at least by doing the DNCB I'm doing something now, and you've given me something to work with."

"I think you'll find that the DNCB might actually help,

and make you feel better," Yale said, "and I'm going to stick around to see that it does. Or, I should say, to see it when it does."

"Positive thinking," Peter said, making a wry face.

"Exactly," Yale agreed cheerfully. "That's half the battle. Positivism. So, I can expect to see you at the next AIDS group, can't I?"

Peter had correctly given the impression that he found the group, as he did all groups, contemptible. But he also knew that at the moment his only true friends were people who had AIDS.

"I'll be there," Peter answered, "if you will."

Being in Oregon now was part of a purification plan that constantly went on in his life. He was always leaving one thing for another, letting the bad effects of situations be soothed away by the constant alteration of environment. This was to lead to an eventual plateau where no one place he lived in could take away any of his self-identity or inner peace. The purpose for being in Oregon could work both ways — one: it afforded him a safe place to die, or two: it provided an opportunity to heal. If Yale's sincerity was authentic, Peter had an intuition that this stranger was not going to let him fade off so easily, and that perhaps together they could make the magic work.

As a child the sound of traffic outside a bedroom window had soothing and calming effects on Peter, as soothing as crickets might have on a city person. When he had visited his grandmother's house it was near a freeway. He loved the excitement of riding in a car at night. As a child, at home with his parents, it was quiet, and there were no neighbors in the forest region where they lived, not far from where his parents lived today.

As he lay awake that night, alone after Yale had brought him home, the thing that kept Peter from sleeping was his memory of New York. Perhaps it had to do with meeting a potential friend in a place where he knew no one except his parents. It gave him the courage to think that perhaps he was glad the whole social bar life he'd led up until that point was over, that there weren't so many areas for growth in that field — that is, as a professional social person, a nobody. He thought, not only are there no promotions in that career, but you either become A: an alcoholic, B: a drug addict, C: sexually compulsive, or D: insensitive. It wasn't that he preferred dying to going back to how it was in New York, but he had decided that in sex — for one thing — he'd had his last mate, or that if he ever did it again it would be because he'd grown fond enough of him to desire having sex. But Peter was just a little impatient with "love," and he never understood what it meant except that it was supposed to be inspirational and that you thought a lot about a person. He knew it was a good thing, that it was one of life's treats. But all he knew about the general topic of love, or romantic relations, was that "love" was something people who were bored wanted and didn't have. It was a word that had been robbed of all meaning as far as he was concerned; he thought that by using the word people could get away with murder.

He resolved that tomorrow he would call Yale up, ask him for more DNCB. The little he'd given him to take home Peter had forgotten to refrigerate, and already it had evaporated on his kitchen counter. He would also find out Yale's thoughts on the subject of love. Peter had never been *in* love. The new panic concerning the tumor on his lip would have to wait for another night; he was now far too tired.

5

Turn around so that the light hits your book." His mother was out in the yard near Peter, picking grapes from the arbor and standing in the sun.

"I'll think about it," he said, trying not to smile.

"This is your mother speaking," she went on playfully.

"Yes, I know, that's why I'm thinking about it first."

She patted his knee.

He looked up in mock irritation. "Off with you," he said.

She continued to fill a white ceramic jug with big bunches of grapes that had turned sweet over night. Peter was spending the afternoon up at his parent's house. Their next door neighbors from across the lake had come over for breakfast. Peter avoided these people and in general only came up when he knew there were no guests.

"Did you think I might refuse to see him?" Peter asked, still looking at the book he was reading.

"Who? Your Dad?"

"No, I meant Yale."

"Yale?"

"The young man from my AIDS group."

"No, I didn't think that, but I did think you might be difficult about it, and that's why I had Sara call you."

"Yes, I know," he said, putting down his book. "Now Sara knows I have AIDS."

His mother continued to pick off the grapes as they talked. "She's mature."

"I guess it's better this way," he said, relenting. "Well, anyway, yesterday I had a very nice time. Yale gave me some medication."

"Your father said he saw a bottle in your kitchen that looked peculiar."

"You know, Dad has absolutely no conception of what's going on with AIDS or anything else."

"That's not true," his mother said in a kindly way that annoyed him.

"But Mom," he answered hotly, "what about mandatory testing legislation and the government's right to the names of those infected, with an eye to quarantine? Dad still refuses to believe that Republican senators have suggested bills to do this. He thinks I'm reading it in the *National Enquirer.* He doesn't understand that the underground press catches these things before the general public does. Gay rights advocates are aware of these things."

"Your father's whole life has been about denial," she said, peeling the skin off one of the grapes with her teeth and eating it. "He denied that he had a drinking problem; he's denied a lot of things. And one of them could easily be that you really have AIDS and might die, or that he voted for a president who's not doing his job." She spat the seeds into her palm.

"I know he'd think I was totally absurd if I wanted to go to the AIDS March on Washington in October," Peter said, closing his book. "He wouldn't understand that the government isn't providing money for a cure, that the President's AIDS committee is made up of antihomosexuals whose report isn't even to be turned in until the President is out of office. Dad wouldn't understand the problem with the FDA not approving or making legal more AIDS treatment therapies. This whole epidemic could have been avoided if Ronald Reagan had acted when AIDS was first brought to the nation's attention six or seven years ago in 1980. Even I know about this stuff."

He was angry, and his mother knew enough to say nothing at all to provoke him. Besides, she was a feminist and their views seldom clashed. She only got mad at him because he hadn't voted in the last election. "Then you have no right to complain," she'd said.

"The main problem I have with your father," she said, to make things lighter between them, "is that he makes too much noise when he eats."

"It's disgusting, isn't it?" he agreed, laughing.

Unlike Peter, his mother believed that society was changing and learning to accept the homosexual. She didn't know if she should completely believe him when he said that because of AIDS violence against homosexuals was on the upswing in the major cities. She thought that homosexuals had nothing but the nation's sympathy.

She went back inside the house and Peter knew she was returning to a book she'd left open somewhere, with her glasses holding down the page. She would come out later, walk into the garden, pick off a few dead flowers, pull up a few weeds, hold her face up to the sun.

They had now achieved a fond compatibility with each other. In fact, as Peter sat in the yard reading his book, he didn't know which was harder to accept, the notion of his death or hers. The world would be a strange and hostile place without the knowledge that his mother was in it.

He looked at his parents' house. He could see the studio light in the basement where Sara lived. She hadn't come out to see him all day, and this upset him, no matter what his mother could assure him about Sara. He simply didn't know if he was strong enough to handle Sara's rejection, either.

"Sara never had a chance to grow up," his mother explained when she came back outside later. "Her adolescence was dominated by your father's worst drinking period."

"But what I can't understand," Peter said, "is why she can't talk to me anymore. We used to be such good friends. Then she found my diary, and read in it that I was gay. . .and went to you. After that she wouldn't be my friend. But I wasn't wrong, she was. She betrayed me."

"In her mind," his mother explained, "she thinks you betrayed her, by being gay. She had other ideas, I guess."

"Well, too bad for her," Peter said, drawing up his shoulders. "This is how things are."

"Neither of you can feel trust for one another," she said wistfully. "It's so sad, really."

"It's sad," he said, "because she's denying herself a brother, and whether she knows it or not, I am a special person."

"That's why you should help her."

But he couldn't. Part of him refused to.

"You know that I had a very special relationship with my mother," she said, sitting next to him and taking up his hand. "I wanted to have the same relationship with my daughter."

"Is that why you spoil her?" he asked.

"Perhaps."

She stroked his hair.

"Sara used to brag about that," he said, "that she had you around her thumb."

"Well, she doesn't," his mother said, but both she and Peter knew it was true.

"I used to be jealous of that," he said.

"I think she felt — with you never calling or coming home, not giving us the right to be your parents — that you forfeited any special attention. She felt she deserved it all."

"But look at her," he said, harshly. "She's such a cripple. She's so repressed."

"I did everything I could," his mother defended herself. "I could have done things so much differently when you two were growing up. But I didn't think I had the strength. Maybe

I would have made a better parent if I'd done it all alone, without your father. But I didn't think I could do it after my mother died. What am I to do about it now? Just enjoy what I have and know that it could have been worse?"

"But that's an awful way to live," he argued, "thinking that it could have been worse."

She smiled sadly and went back inside again to her book. Peter was sad now too, and he was tired. He walked down the trail to his cottage to take a nap.

I don't want my mother to be alone, he thought later as he lay in bed. In dying he was leaving her like a preschool child being left for the first time in the care of a teacher in a classroom with other children, all of them making an equal fuss. He didn't want to separate from his mother forever. "If there is a heaven," his mother had said, "think of the good company we'll be in." He wanted to believe her. He wanted to believe that his Grandmother would be there. She must be there, he thought, if there is a "There."

One of the particular problems that the concept of heaven posed was how everyone would appear? He decided that people would be allowed to choose for themselves, and they would probably all choose to appear young, in their prime. This of course would make it difficult for some who remembered great-grandparents, but it would probably be a good, healthy situation where everyone would be equal. Of course, there could also be the possibility that everyone would appear to the people who knew them on earth as they'd looked then. But he knew this was all in the mind. Death was something far grander, the mixing of energies and spirits, the rejuvenating of life.

The parties and happenings he had dreaded most or been so afraid of (like swimming lessons and jumping off the diving board at the deep end) had always been better than he'd anticipated. There was no reason death should be any different, but that didn't mean he'd not fight against it: his life was a half-finished project, and half-finished projects were disgraceful.

As the afternoon shortened, he started thinking about other things . . .

He rolled over in bed and reached inside the drawer of his night table and took out a sheet of paper. On it he began writing a letter to his mother, which he planned to place in her bedroom so that someday she would find it.

Dear Mom,

The other night you told me that when Grandma died you always regretted not being there to tell me. You were sorry that Dad took it upon himself. I was sorry, too, because I needed at that moment to be told by you, and I needed it to be you, not him. When I was diagnosed with AIDS it was Dad I talked to on the phone — you weren't home. It was like talking to a cardboard person, a telephone operator, and at the second most tragic moment. I never blamed you for this because it was only coincidence. But I want to ask you something very important and probably it's not the right time but I have to ask it anyway: if anything happens to me and I do die, I want you to be there at that moment. Don't let it be him. I needed compassion at those two other times. I didn't get any. Dying in his presence is the thing I dread most.

I know my being sick is a sacrifice for Dad to have to make, because he must relinguish you a little bit to me. I know he feels helpless when you love me because he feels shut out. And maybe he has a right as your husband to feel that way, but I think he must learn to be a little less selfish right now, because I'm dying. It's hard for him to sacrifice; he doesn't even like to see me get the largest helpings at dinner. But I would like to see him learn that it is not healthy for him to be so dependent on you. I also don't want to let him deny me your support, which I need.

I love you more than anyone and if you died before me it wouldn't be any easier than this. If I can't trust any one, I know I can always trust you.

Love, Peter.

He put down the pencil and paper. A gigantic worry was out of his mind. His thoughts began to wander. Eventually they settled on Yale.

6

Sara was sitting on a deck chair. It was twilight and Peter had just awakened from his nap. It was also the beginning of fall. The lawns had been mowed and raked for the winter; the small boats were pulled up onto the dock or hoisted out of the water. But there was still warmth, barely, and Sara was sitting in the cold sun, conscious as everyone was that it would be one of the last good days of the year.

Peter saw her from the kitchen. He breathed deeply, and just when it was easy to do nothing, to ignore, to deny as Sara and his father did so well, he marched out onto the patio and wordlessly sat down beside her.

"Dad wants you to pay Mom back the money you borrowed from her," Sara said finally. "I don't understand what business that is of his. But that's what he told me, and so I'm just telling you." Her face remained strangely impassive.

Peter looked at her, but he could see no emotion in her face. It frightened him. "Well," he said gently, "at least he was able to talk to you about something other than real estate." (He knew that later he would have the chance to be angry with his father, to be furious, in fact. But even to react now would be low. His father's words were only the remarks of an impatient man.) Peter was trying to figure out his sister, but he wouldn't budge. However, it was obvious she was not going to talk about AIDS.

"Isn't it fun staying here?" Sara asked sarcastically.

He could remember a time when his sister used to hate
their father. Now, in the end, she still mocked him but she
was going to deny, to avoid. Except for the time when their
grandmother died many years ago he'd never seen her cry.
It was a turning point in his family. Where tragedy had
opened Peter up, it had closed up his sister. She was one of
his bigger disappointments. But Peter was convinced that
unlike their father, somewhere deep within, Sara had feelings
and that intuitively she understood it was not a good thing
to lose her brother, even if she couldn't show it. He thanked
God for his mother's feelings. Otherwise his life would be too
horrible.

The fact that Peter's father was retired was unfortunate.
It meant that he was around the house all the time, sitting
at the big window with a clear view of the caretaker's
cottage, working endlessly at jigsaw puzzles.

At the same time, Peter and Sara looked up and saw their father
coming down the trail towards them. Peter believed that he
could see his sister's body tense up. She lit a cigarette.

"Your mother went over to town," their father told them.

"So we're stuck with you, then?" Sara said so that only
Peter could hear her.

Peter smiled.

It was true that Sara was one of the few people who could
make him laugh outright. It was often that way with family
members: they share a common sense of humor. In Peter's
family, ridicule and sarcasm were the general forms. They
learned it from their mother, who communicated with
sarcasm for several terrible years when her husband was drinking heavily.

Peter's father was a stupid drunk, and it annoyed
everyone. They made fun of him. But it was the only way
they could cope. Today, Sara and Peter were closest when she

made a sly remark about their father. In high school she and
Peter had been popular because they both had the nerve to
poke fun at their teachers. Like Peter's mother, Sara had the
ability to make her father feel inadequate. But Peter didn't trust
Sara's sympathies; he knew that when he wasn't there Sara
and her father got along very well. Yet by making fun of their
father, Sara was obviously trying to communicate with Peter.
He and his father were old enemies who had learned now
to live peacefully together. Sara knew how to get at everyone,
but right now Peter wasn't going to let her.

"Do you want to take the motorboat out?" their father
asked.

Sara would have to say something quickly, merely to
pause was to debase him.

"I think it's too windy," she said.

Silently, dejectedly, their father went to the boathouse.

"You blew your opportunity," Sara chided, but Peter
didn't smile. Disappointing an old man gave him no joy. Yet
to go to his father now would seem as if he were pitying him,
and Peter's father was sensitive to that.

"Do you still have a boyfriend?" Peter asked.

When Peter was home several years ago, a young man,
athletic and opinionated, visited her. Peter hated him but had
never told anyone except his mother. "I think it would be
very bad if they got married," his mother once said. "Sara told
me she'd thought about marrying but Greg didn't want to. I'm
afraid he'll just walk away from her one day, when she's not
twenty-three anymore, when she's thirty." When he heard this,
Peter had several reactions. One was surprise that his sister
could make such an emotional statement, such a commitment
as wanting to marry anyone. But more than his surprise at
this, he was outraged that anyone would ever turn his sister
down. How dare they? Would the rejection wake her up —
wake up the Sara who had rejected everyone around her? That
anyone would ever say no to his sister did upset Peter. He

hoped the jolt would wake her up. Perhaps she had woken up to it, but because of the past maybe she found it difficult to open up suddenly to a brother she had kept at a distance for so long. Perhaps it was more his fault. On the other hand, because of the past, Peter found it necessary that it be Sara who made the first overture; Peter wasn't willing to be snubbed. It would hurt as it always had, and he couldn't bear that — not then and particularly not now.

Sara answered his question: "Greg still comes over a lot. He stays up at the house."

Peter remembered that when he was home before, Greg seemed always to stand behind Sara, as if protecting himself from exposure to Peter. What did Peter stand for to this stranger — a bizarre homosexual? This tried his patience. How many battles had he already fought to prove he was normal — a battle he was still fighting with Sara, a battle his father no longer engaged in. Peter's mother simply loved him, no questions necessary. And now that he had AIDS? Double degenerate. What more could he do to make things better with Sara? Nothing. All he could do was what he was doing now, sitting with her and in so doing saying: I want more than just a placid acceptance. I want you to talk to me.

"Doesn't Dad drive you crazy?" Sara asked, making conversation, not looking at him but at the lake.

Dad doesn't drive me crazy, Peter could have said, having AIDS drives me crazy. Things are different now, regular things aren't important anymore.

But for Sara to acknowledge this she would have to acknowledge his tragedy. Would she only deal with it at his funeral? Yes, then she'd mourn, then she'd regret. If he could, he'd make it easier for her, but he couldn't do anything as long as she denied.

He wanted to be alone now. Sara made him nervous. She hadn't said anything about his AIDS and he knew she never would. This isn't a very valuable relationship, he thought somewhat bitterly. He knew that if he said anything about homosexuality or AIDS she would be so on edge that she would stand up and move away. All right, he thought, I'll play it your way.

He watched his sister light another cigarette. They could hear the motorboat starting up, then it pulled out of the boathouse and his father, without looking at them, headed out toward the middle of the lake. Peter felt sick inside. Flicking her cigarette into the lake, Sara, indifferent, got up and walked away.

Letting himself go limp, Peter lay back on the cool grass and looked at the clouds. They were the same clouds he knew as a child, and by concentrating as he once had, he was able to imagine that it was only the earth turning and the clouds that were standing still.

DNCB was not a painless drug, Yale had told him. The objective in taking it was to cause a reaction, an irritation to stimulate the T-cells and at the same time work on the disease. The lotion that Peter applied to the lesions on his body, alone in his bedroom, stung less than the regular liquid that went along with the overall treatment. But was he being overly anxious to imagine that the drug was already working, making him feel better, more powerful, like his old self — whatever that was. When had he ever felt really strong? He could remember as a kid feeling indestructible. He got over colds more quickly than he usually thought he would, when he scraped his knee it healed fast. Secretly he felt that he was really stronger than most other people. But he'd outsmarted himself – he wasn't stronger. Now he was weaker.

He didn't have the heart to look at his legs – it seemed like every day there was a new lesion waiting for him. One of these days his whole body would become one great bloody purple splotch.

He got up and looked out the window at the lake. He could see his father's boat drawn up beside the lake patrol. He and the officer were talking.

Am I going to live? It was a question Peter was hesitant to answer. To say that he would could be avoiding the truth, to say that he wouldn't could actually be preventing positive thinking. It was a toss-up certainly, but he'd try to take his chances with believing that he'd live. Why not? Yes, why not?

His mouth hurt; he had something called hairy leukoplakia, which were white sores on his tongue. They seemed to be multiplying. What could he tell himself? Certainly he wasn't falling down in the street like some of his friends had. It was also true that getting up in the morning was hard, the way it was when he'd had monster hangovers. But he had to avoid getting overexcited about these things. The calm before the storm. That was another dangerous but understandable perception that had to still be avoided. "Just don't let me deny," he said out loud. "I can't afford to do that. Some people I know can, I can't."

The lesions on his face had seemed to go down since taking the DNCB Yale had given him. That was good, but did it mean the virus was leaving him or was DNCB only a cosmetic answer? It wasn't actually supposed to be.

There were times he wanted a drink but he wasn't an alcoholic like his father. Then what was he? Alcohol had been an answer in the past. He laughed. How am I different from Sara? Sara criticized their father but she was no different — incapable as he of emotion, of confrontation. Was he not confronting by thinking he wasn't or hadn't been an alcoholic? Did it matter?

Alcohol . . . No, it hadn't been an answer. He never relied on it for that, and in that way it had never let him down. Alcohol only made time pass more easily. Wasn't there a song by James Taylor that his roommate in New York had often quoted: "The secret of life is enjoying the passage of time"?

Take a deep breath, Peter. Take down the mirrors. Stop thinking too much. Look to nature (that thought made him gag). But there's got to be another way. This is the answer — only look in the mirror once a day; you haven't changed, the body is only physical, it isn't all spiritual. Too much thinking. One of these days he would have to control it.

He looked out at the lake and saw his father's boat heading toward their dock.

Peter washed his face in the sink. Then he went outside to wait for his father. When he came back to the dock, Peter was standing there with the rope to tie the boat up. He helped his father bring the boat in.

"When is Mom coming back?" Peter asked. The question was for his father's benefit. Peter knew that his father, since giving up alcohol, hated to be alone. When he received no answer, Peter said abruptly: "Mom needs to get out of the house more often."

"I let her do what she wants." His father busied himself picking up the trash from the boat.

Peter was disappointed; he felt his father wasn't being honest again. He'd long since forfeited any right to comment on his wife's behavior and they both knew it. There were too many nights when Peter's father had not come home at all, too many years relying on his wife's inheritance money instead of making some for himself. If anything Peter's father was lucky; most women with just a little more self-assurance would have dumped him.

But in order to talk to his father Peter had to play along, had to let him try to give the impression that he had been a success in life. In his life Peter had gone out of his way to be different; he knew that truth only opened more avenues.

"Mom told me she thinks you look sick," Peter said, making an attempt. "She said it when I first came home. You don't want to see a doctor?"

Peter suspected cancer. His father was gray and looked

much older than his mother. They were the same age. He looked frail and bitter and Peter remembered his mother once telling him over the phone in New York that his father had frequent problems breathing, that once he'd curled up on the lawn, unable to breathe. "The only way I could get him to move," his mother had said, "was by shouting at him and saying: 'You're not going to die on my lawn.' " She had driven him to the hospital. "He acts as if he had nothing to live for anymore." The truth was that his father has always been lazy; he only did things to get acknowledgement, initially from his own mother and then from his wife. It was not enough to wash a window; he had to point out that he'd done it so that his wife could, in essence, tell him that he was good.

"Your mother will do fine without me," Peter's father said without prompting. But Peter wasn't asking his father for confidences. Peter just wanted truth.

"If I die," his father said, "she doesn't have to make any more compromises. She can watch whatever she wants to on television, run things the way she wants to, she can go her own way. She put everything in her name a long time ago. I don't care."

But, of course, he did care and Peter knew it. "Dad," he said, "Mom would be lonely without you. She'd miss you."

"I don't know about that," he said.

Does he really believe it? Peter wondered.

"People never know how they'll really react to anything until it actually happens," Peter said. "I know Mom would miss you."

His father looked confused. "I'm going to take a hot bath," he said.

Peter watched him go.

Once more Peter was alone. He went back into his house, took off his shirt and looked in the mirror. By staring hypnotically at the lesion on his abdomen he was going to pretend that he was making it shrink.

7

He looked across the room. Yale, smirking, was seated next to several people. Although members of the AIDS group were not exactly discouraged from meeting outside, there were strict rules about sexual or intimate activity.

"Not until after a year," the social worker had urged. People have imaginations and this fact wasn't lost on Yale and Peter. Without saying a word to each other about it, both of them had decided to play it cool in front of the others.

"My T-cell count was 800 last year," one of the members was saying. "Now it's under 100. I can't help thinking that it's just so unfair.

"You shared that before," the social worker reminded him.

"But I still feel it," the young man insisted. "I'm glad to be here," he went on, "because it's good to hear about other people's experiences with AZT and interferon. My family and friends say, 'Hang in there.' I get tired of that, it's sort of like saying, 'Have a good day.' "

Someone else spoke, I haven't been having much success either. When I get depressed I just get high."

"You're back to that, too," another asked.

Peter was so late he'd missed most of the group's discussion. He could tell that Yale had already spoken. This frustrated him. He couldn't help but wonder if in talking about his past week Yale had mentioned having met Peter, that they had

become friends. When it was Peter's turn to talk he wondered
how he'd get around it. He wondered if he'd even bother to
talk. Part of him didn't want to be part of the group. Yale was
all he needed as a friend; he didn't need a group of people.

"It must be hard for all of you," the social worker was
saying. "There's all these drugs to keep track of, all these
initials, and who knows which ones are good for you or not."

"Go for the ones that have no side effects," Peter
volunteered, surprised at himself for speaking out. Yale shot
him a glance.

"Sometimes," one of the members said, "I wonder if I'd
be less sick if I'd never take AZT in the first place. I just seem
to be getting sicker. My doctor says if I quit interferon now
I'll die. If I understand him correctly, I've built up a depend-
ency on it. My body couldn't handle this onslaught of germs
if I dropped AZT. But my body is completely sore from
injecting the interferon into my muscles. I don't know how
much longer I can take it. But I'm not going to argue with
him. I can't afford to be wrong, to take the risk that I'd die
if I went off the drugs. It's a gamble I can't take."

Peter was glad he'd never taken AZT, because of the side
effects and glad because he didn't want to have to depend on
any one thing forever. Things and people both have a tendency
to betray you – you can't count on anything. In other words, he
thought, I'm not going to put all of my eggs in one basket.

"What should we talk about next?" the social worker asked.

"Sex," someone suggested.

"Good topic." The social worker leaned forward. "How
do you people feel about sex now that you have AIDS?"

Peter couldn't help himself; he looked over at Yale. As
people began to discuss their feelings, their fears about physical
intimacy, Peter shut down. He was angry. I'm not going to
talk about this in front of a group of strangers, he thought.
But the truth was that Yale's presence now intimidated him.
To consider sex at all at this point was to confront his feel-

ings about his friendship with Yale. He wasn't ready.

When the meeting was over and as each member hugged one another, Peter waited until it was all over before he hugged Yale.

"How are you?" Yale asked in a conspiratorial voice. "Do you want to go somewhere for coffee?"

They were standing on the lawn in front of the social worker's house.

"Let's go to your place," Peter said, "We can talk better."

"So, what do your parents think about your being gay?" Yale asked, once they were alone in his apartment.

"My Mom doesn't seem any different toward me since she's known. Maybe we're even closer." Peter settled back on Yale's bed, took off his shoes and pushed aside the classified section of the newspaper.

"And your Dad?"

"Well, I know he doesn't like gay people," Peter said. "I can remember him making remarks about them. He doesn't like black people. He doesn't like Jews. Why should he like gays? We don't discuss it. It's just one more thing we don't discuss. The only thing to discuss with him is real estate. Every once in a while we talk about other things. The other day he admitted he might be very ill. I guess that was a start. But he didn't go very far. I don't think he even knows what the truth is about anything. He never did. The truth would destroy him. But I suppose he does know the truth and that's his problem: he's a failure in his own eyes. So to cover it up he lives in a world of complete and total fantasy. He pretends that it was his money and not my Mom's that we've lived on all these years."

"Are you a failure? It's a fair question," Yale reminded him. He sat next to Peter on the bed. "I have a direct way of asking questions. You can evade all you want."

"No, I don't think I'm a failure," Peter said gently, beginning to smile. "Are you a failure?"

"Sometimes I think I am," Yale said. "I had plans.

Getting AIDS didn't wreck those plans. I wouldn't have written a book anyway."

"You're really trying to write one?" Peter looked at him.

"I'm not even trying," Yale answered. "I thought if I talked about it enough it would just write itself and appear next to my bed someday."

"Next to your bed?"

"That's where I do most of my thinking."

"I always think," Peter said, "except when I'm talking."

"What do you think about?" Yale asked.

Peter stared at the floor. He felt embarrassed.

"Do you ever think about love?" Yale asked.

"Never," Peter said a little too quickly. Love only meant despair. It was like any drug. Now that Yale had brought up the subject Peter felt stifled.

"How do you feel about it now that you have AIDS?"

"I don't think about love now at all," Peter said. "I wonder if I'm even going to be around to eat breakfast or brush my teeth."

"Do you avoid love because the general population tells us that homosexual acts are courting death?"

"No, Yale," he laughed, "don't be stupid. It has to do with emotions."

"I think love is important, but I'm a little inclined to believe you. I think it's a lot of hogwash in the first place. I know there are gay relationships that work, but who can say what they're like?"

"Maybe it's not our place to have relationships," Peter said. "Maybe we're supposed to be the observers. Maybe our lives function as a role in a way we don't understand."

"It's entirely possible," Yale said, "but I just don't know. Politics make a lot more sense to me. They're tangible. When you lived in New York and California, what did you believe in?"

Peter made a funny expression with his mouth. "You're not going to believe it," he said.

"Try me," Yale answered.

"Stupid things: sex, drugs, and loud music."

"Oh." Yale looked discouraged.

"It was enough for me," Peter explained. "It didn't leave me time for much else, and by not doing these things people didn't feel any more or less than I did. It was a roller coaster all the time, and my head is still spinning a little bit, but not too much."

"So what's next?" Yale asked.

"First," Peter said screwing up his eyes, "I have to figure out how not to die. Remember, that's what you're going to help me with, with your information about drug protocols. After that? Who knows? Maybe I'll be so happy I'll want to fall in love."

"Impossible." Yale straightened a stack of newspapers.

"Impossible, why?" Peter laughed. He could tell that Yale was uneasy.

"Impossible because you're just like me."

"But you could change, too." Peter stared at him. He wrinkled his brow. "Maybe we could change together."

Yale stood up. He was looking for a cigarette and a match. He found the matches first.

"What's wrong?" Peter asked, touched and confused at once.

"It's just that I think you're very attractive," Yale blurted out.

Peter took this in stride. "I've thought the same of you," he said. "And I've thought about you, too. But that's not what's important anymore. I've spent too much time sleeping with people and then hoping a friendship would come out of it. Now if sex happens at all, it's going to have to come out of a friendship that's already been established. Friendship has got to come first. The natural result of feelings that have developed."

"So I'm not the only intellectual here," Yale said.

"You get this way after you've lived in all the big gay meccas."

"I've lived in them, too," Yale said. "And I'm here for the same reasons you are. I'm here somewhat permanently but I wasn't born here."

"I'm very excited about living here with my parents again," Peter said. "I can't walk out of this world without coming back here. My mother meant a great deal to me once and she still does and I can't leave her without saying a proper goodbye."

"Is that what you're doing?"

"I'm doing a lot of things," he said. "I'm trying to become a person again."

"I think you're just fine as a person, Peter." Yale reached over and kissed Peter on the cheek.

Startled, Peter's face turned pink. "I think you're doing well yourself," he said awkwardly.

"I just had a phone call yesterday from New York," Yale said, sitting down again. "Three more people I know are dead."

"I know," Peter said. "I haven't called anyone. I'm afraid to. I'm so worried for a couple of my friends. I know Stephen has only one or two people left in his social circle, all of his other friends are gone. It's almost too scary to believe, but you have to."

"Who's going to be left in a couple of years? Any of our friends?"

"None of our gay ones. I don't even know if we will be."

"Sobering, isn't it?"

"Too," Peter said.

"I wonder if becoming a Christian would help?"

"It won't stop our friends from dying, that's all I know." Peter wanted to lie down. Talking like this made him feel as though he'd downed a glass of bitter ale. "Do you ever plan, in the bottom of your heart, to leave here?" he asked. "To go back to one of the big cities? Or is this home? How permanent do you feel about this place?"

"They say that when people come to Portland they

usually don't leave. You're more from here than I am, Peter, and maybe that's why I feel more like staying than you might. You know Portland. The East Coast is still a challenge to you, it's not so much to me. Although I come originally from Miami Beach."

"The Bronx in mink."

"What?"

"I heard it somewhere."

"If I'm going to die," Yale concluded, "I'm going to do it here."

"Die in Oregon?" A bleakness rushed through Peter. He knew that if he was to die it would never be in Portland. It would have to be in New York City, on a crowded street, with his boots on, so to speak.

"But you don't live badly. Look at your parents, Peter. Why would you want to die in squalor?"

"I don't want to die in squalor," Peter said. "I just don't want to be broke, living in a welfare hotel. I also don't want to die in obscurity; I want to be a part of what's happening. That's New York, it's not Portland."

"So why not go back to New York right now?"

"I can't. I don't know if I ever can. I don't have the strength; it would wipe me out overnight."

"Overnight? So go to sleep then."

"I didn't mean one night of partying. I just meant I'd go quickly."

"I think I have your number," Yale said. "You're hopeless."

"It's true. But look at how I'm living now. I'm happy – a cottage with big empty rooms, tall windows looking out on a lake. There's lots of peace."

"You're just getting ready for something. You just want to get well so you can go back to killing yourself."

"How penetrating, Yale. But maybe it's not true. Can't I change like everybody else?"

"If it makes you feel better I'll say it: you can change."

"And I have your number," Peter said. "You're being bitter and disillusioned – you didn't get to do all you wanted, you got AIDS. So now here you are, the world has treated you unfairly. I think that's very boring."

Yale looked crestfallen.

"Listen," Peter said. "I have my doubts about why I'm really here now, when I could be with my friends in New York."

"Your house," Yale said, making an effort now to reassure him, "functions as a retreat — use it for that. When you forget why you're here, remember — it's only for that."

"Thanks, Yale. You're right. It's not supposed to be anything more than that. It's not a coffin."

"Do you think the DNCB did you any good?"

"I don't know," Peter said. "All I know is that it leaves red marks from the liquid and the ointment I put on the lesions."

"You're going to have an actual sore with the liquid," Yale warned him, "but that's what you want – a reaction so the T-cells can be stimulated."

"I need some more of the liquid," Peter said.

"I try to imagine that it's working, and I don't think I'm dying as quickly, but that might only be because I stopped cocaine and alcohol. Who knows?"

"That's the worst part — nobody does. I'm just glad we're both not on AZT. Not only are my friends getting blood transfusions for the red cells, but they're losing white and you can't put those back in. Thank God AZT isn't the only way; it's turning out to be detrimental. But despite what I've been taking I still feel a little weak lately. It's hard to be a powerhouse of hope."

Peter took Yale's hand. "From now on," he said, "I want you to call me. No matter what's happening, okay? Let's talk every day. Do you promise?"

Yale reached over and gave Peter a hug. Peter could feel Yale's fingers digging into him. Peter held on as tightly as he could.

8

Peter gave little philosophical speeches as a child when he was alone. Then it was a TV show, with an imaginary camera trained on him. He felt that what he was doing was wrong, that if he were overheard he would be ridiculed. He began to hide things; sexual arousal was just one of them.

He also didn't know when he first became a liar. Today he wasn't a liar: lying in the past had been an aid to getting what he wanted, and got what he needed now, so there was no need for it. But in the beginning he hadn't known that. He supposed that the first memory he had of commiting a sin was the time he told his first grade teacher that he was moving to Canada. He said it because another school chum had said the very same thing and then actually done it. Peter wanted people to appreciate him, too. So he told the lie that he was moving, and for a solid week he had everyone's attention. His teacher finally called home to verify Peter's departure date. When Peter came home that day his father was waiting for him with an empty suitcase that he told Peter to fill.

The next big lie came not much later. A school bus had overturned in the snow. Peter told the kids that he had been on that bus. During the morning discussion group one of Peter's friends volunteered this information to the teacher. She said it was a school bus full of black children who were being sent to segregated schools. Peter had been caught again.

It was ironic for Peter to note that when he informed his friends he had AIDS he got the reaction that he would have wanted as a first grader, and in so doing he now felt that same guilt.

One night after dinner, he and his mother were alone and watching the sun set. It was a big red disk — and had been so for two nights — as a result of the smog from forest fires in southern Oregon. "Do you remember that black man, Will, the consultant, who used to come around the house when Dad was so drunk?" Peter asked. "You and Will would sit talking and he flirted with you. Did that humiliate Dad?"

"Will was a con man, but he was always very sweet to me," his mother answered. "The sheriff was over here one day after Will disappeared, and it seems that Will had a rap sheet a mile long. He swindled rich ladies. Will admitted that to me one day in the very beginning. When I was threatening your father with a divorce, your father was scared, since the money was all mine. His friends got Will to come over, because your father thought that if Will and I had an affair he could prove in court that I was an unfit mother. Then he could get custody of you and Sara."

"Dad thought you were that stupid? Or that you'd do such a thing?"

"I guess so. Can you believe it? I liked Will, no matter how bad he was. Whether I knew his real name or not didn't matter; he was nice to my children and he never once made a pass at me. One day he came over and said: 'Do you really want to know where your husband is right now?' He dialed the number of a woman in Dunthorpe. I could just see it — a middle-aged woman in lingerie, the curtains drawn, a glass of scotch in her hand. Your father got on the phone and I listened to them talk. Will was my friend; he helped me. He didn't use me."

"So how can you still feel love for Dad?"

"It's different, that's all. It's hard for me to be intimate

with him today, but we get along compatibly. I know he loves
me. He does whatever I tell him, but he's not much fun. He
used to be so gregarious. When he goes without alcohol he
never wants to go anywhere; he sits in the corner when guests
come; he doesn't like the symphony. I have to make him go
to things. I have to get the tickets. It's taken a lot of courage
for him to overcome his problem, to admit to the world that
he is a failure, to get up in front of people at that institution
and tell them how he feels. I give him credit for that. It's the
hardest thing he's ever done."

"Still, it's hard to have sympathy," Peter said.

"What about me? How many times did we go to the
grocery store together, where strangers would say hello to him
and they'd talk? Then I'd ask your father who they were and
he'd say, 'I don't know.' He'd never want to introduce me to
them. You see, he had a whole other secret world."

The sky was now broken up into layers of purple and
blue.

"In grade school," Peter said, "the other kids were always
jealous and envious of me because my father was so friendly
and nice. But it was so ironical, because actually he was so
horrible. They never knew that – and when I'd tell them they'd
never believe me."

"Nobody believed me when I said he was an alcoholic,
either," his mother said. "It wasn't until he was bouncing off
the walls and people were laughing at him that they started
to understand. They thought I was out of my mind when I
found his car at a condo in Troutdale and let the air out of
his tires. I even wanted to hire a private detective. It's better
now, I suppose. But he follows me from room to room, always
asking me where I'm going to sit. It drives me bananas."

"I just don't know why you stayed married."

"I was afraid. I didn't think I could be a single parent."

"Oh, well, it doesn't matter now, does it?"

"I hope you don't blame me too much."

"I don't, Mom." He gave her a hug. "You had to take care of yourself, too." They sat motionless for a long while and listened to the crickets. It was dark now. "Mom, you know how most parents worry about what's going to become of their kids after they're dead and not there to protect them? Well, it can also go the other way. I worry about what's going to happen to you after Dad is gone. I don't think you can rely on Sara for continued emotional support."

"I don't know, either," his mother said. Peter could tell it was a raw issue for her as well. "I have a hard enough time being intimate with your father anymore; I can't trust people easily. It takes me years to make friends. And look what's happened to all the women I know. When Louis divorced Helen and married someone else, it killed her."

She died of cancer, Peter said to himself, and the cancer was Louis, who had ruined her life. Louis should be in a monastery praying. Helen was the strongest woman Peter knew, and that was the point: what was going to happen to his mother? "I don't think Cynthia is really happy, either."

"She's sleeping with her psychiatrist. I just can't do those things. I never will."

"I don't want you to have to, Mom."

"Are you still interested in going to the beach? I've rented a house for the four of us."

"I think that would be very nice," Peter said, "just like we used to do when Sara and I were growing up. It's a very good idea."

"Do you remember, when you were a little boy, you used to tell me, 'Mom, when I grow up we'll have a big house and we'll live in it together?'"

"I'd still do it, if I could."

Would I have gotten AIDS if I had come back to my mother's world sooner? he wondered silently. Is disability the reward for my courage?

"Mom," he said aloud, "from here on out we'll take care

of each other."

Peter's father passed through the room. "I'm watching television up in the bedroom," he said, trying to draw her away from Peter. She remained still until he had left the room.

"I wish you could have known him when I first met him," she said. "He was so debonair. He had such a good way with people. No wonder people today can't understand why I married him; he was so different then. But after we were married he dropped out of law school. I never understood why. Perhaps that was his first mistake. His best friends have all become judges, lawyers, and senators. Your father went into advertising, and from there it was a drunken decline.

"A few years ago I made him get a job. Do you know what he did? He was a security guard. He looked at people's door passes. He convinced himself he was a receptionist. And the very people he worked with as an executive for the Port of Portland were now the same people that he would hold the door for. Then he was sent home from that job for being too drunk. That's when I told him we didn't want him in this family if he drank. Sara was here and she agreed with me. I didn't care how miserable I'd be if I was alone. Nothing could have been worse than living with our father at that point."

"Were there ever any other men in your life?" he asked.

"I dated a doctor once when I was nineteen," she said wistfully. "He was a medical student then. I would have continued to date him but he wanted to break it off because he thought I was too young. He was just starting to study for his degree. He thought it was too early to marry. He wanted to get around a little more first."

"Did that make you unhappy?"

"I was very disappointed."

Peter could feel her hurt.

"Then, a year later I met a young man I really liked. We dated, and then he joined the service. He wrote me letters every week, and when he came home on leave we went out a couple of times. Later I found out he'd come home much earlier than he'd told me. One day he left suddenly. I didn't hear from him at all. I sent him a Christmas card. When he came back for the holidays I read in the newspaper that he was engaged to the girl who lived next door to him."

"Did that make you unhappier than before?"

His mother looked out the window. The sky was completely dark now, but there was a glow of lights from Tigard over the ridge of mountains.

"I had been double-dating with my best friend and her boyfriend – your father, before my boyfriend joined the army. When he got married and my best friend went to Europe to get married, too, your father and I went out — I guess at first to console each other."

At that moment Peter's father passed through the room again into the kitchen. He slammed a cupboard drawer.

"It looks like I'm in trouble," his mother said, poking Peter playfully. "He thinks I should be up there in bed, watching television with him. He feels very nervous when you come up here and steal me away from him."

"Doesn't he have anything to do for himself?"

"Absolutely nothing."

"Whose idea was it to have children anyway?" Peter asked. "Yours? His?"

"Mine. Isn't it obvious? I thought children would act as a buffer, since we weren't getting along, I guess because of his drinking. And as you can see, you kids still act as buffers, and it still doesn't please him."

"Does he love us at all?"

"I think he really does. He couldn't show it, of course. Now I have a question for you, Peter."

"Shoot."

"When you were six years old and I left you with baby-sitters while I went back to the University, did you hate that? Did you feel neglected?"

"I don't even remember."

She sighed. "Shall we watch TV now?"

"I think I might go down to bed." He stood and stretched.

"I thought one of these nights you were going to help me write a mystery novel."

"But not tonight, Mom."

When his mother swore to him that he would not die alone, that his father would not be there, that only she would be holding his hand, Peter also swore to her that if a cure happened tomorrow and he became well again, she would not be alone in her old age, that he would live with her, just as he had once promised. He'd fullfill this promise. Got would be their witness.

"Mommy," he said as he went to the door, "neither one of us will be alone."

She smiled. "Should I turn the trail lights on?"

9

As a child Peter was fascinated by the movement and direction of clouds, which signaled to him the turning of the earth. He watched the sun, which went down, as he learned, in the west. The ocean was to the west, and that was the point into which the sun disappeared. The ocean was the greatest mystery of life. He remembered being frightened when a grown-up said there were holes in the earth: there were places in the sand where the tide broke, where you could fall right through and into inner space. You would keep on falling into eternity. He'd also been told that jellyfish stung. He didn't believe it, but he was unwilling to test one to find out. He also knew there were sharks and whales in the ocean. He knew of sunken treasure, and once, as a very small boy, he even remembered construction cranes digging at one of the beaches after an old map had been found drawn on a rock. Once Peter hid money in the sand, and then told Sara that he'd discovered it.

The sea was scary, but it was also sad and tormented. People were baptised in water, he knew. Water washed away sins; it cleansed. It also spat forth glass floats from Japan, blue or green. The ocean polished glass, too, making its sharp edges smooth. One time he wrote a mysterious message about being a shipwrecked sailor, placed it into a corked bottle, and tossed it in when the tide went out. He knew too that lonely people lived at oceanside, people who were unmarried or

people who had married several times and were once
more alone.

During a storm the ocean could wash away houses. It
could seize anything. There was another world below its
surface. The morning air always smelled of salt. How did the
ocean produce salt? From minerals. But how did it work?

Peter had spent the entire day with Yale before Peter's
family left Portland and drove to Salishan for a vacation. Peter
and Yale went to the Galleria, the Metro Café, and to the
Pioneer Court House to watch the John Reed Day celebration.
Then they walked down to Old Town to look in the shops
and galleries. It was interesting for Peter, but only because Yale
had come with him. He'd asked Yale to come to the beach
with them, but Yale had said no, and Peter couldn't blame
him; he'd never liked going on vacations with other people's
families. It was intimidating.

The day they arrived in Salishan, he wrote Yale a letter.
The old nagging fear came back: would this letter be mailed
if I were to die suddenly? Oh, stop it! he had to remind himself,
you should be so lucky to die, you fool.

When the luggage had been put in the bedrooms upstairs
and the food in the kitchen, Peter and his mother were standing before the large windows looking out at the sea. It
seemed as if the house had been built with only three sides,
the fourth being entirely of glass.

Sara had gone upstairs. Peter's father was already watching
television.

With long coats, scarves, and hats, Peter, and his mother
went out into the stinging wind. The sand was damp and soft,
like a carpet. They had no difficulty climbing down the slope
to the beach.

"Look at all that foam," Peter had to shout. He could smell
charcoal burning. He looked out at the waves. They broke and
then fell like miniature waterfalls.

The pounding of the waves made conversation difficult.

Peter and his mother tried sitting against a log at one point, with their backs to the wind, but even when it let up a bit, there was still sand in the air; it got into Peter's eyes and felt abrasive against his skin. He was curious to know if he'd ever been comfortable at all sitting for long periods beside the ocean. He supposed that as a kid he'd been too busy digging, going back and forth from the water carrying fresh hard sand for whatever he was creating. But he did remember his mother, reading books. Now he found little pleasure in being outside in the sand and wind. This disappointed him; it made him feel like an old man. After all, the ocean was still his favorite thing. What a tremendous force, all that water. He'd always be in awe of it. At the ocean, he felt heaven was closer.

He ran down to the water's edge as he had all his life, dodging the incoming tide, waiting until the last moment to back away quickly without getting his feet wet. He was thinking of the final scene in *Interiors,* when Geraldine Page walked straight into the ocean and drowned.

As Peter and his mother walked, he pictured his father sitting bored before the television, waiting for his wife to return. He seemed to be saying to Peter, "You want to rob me of my position in this family; You want to take away my life. You wish I was dead. I get in the way. I am something you have to work around. Your lives would be less interrupted if I weren't here."

Peter felt horrible. After all, wasn't he really taking his mother away from his father? Wasn't it true that things would be less complicated if his father were gone? "He is just like a little baby," his mother would say. But he was a baby who gave nothing in return. He merely existed, taking up space. Peter was ashamed of this harsh judgment, yet he felt it was true. Should he try to draw more of a boundary between himself and his mother? Was it unhealthy that he, instead of his father, should be sharing her happier moments now? When he told his mother this, she tried to reassure him. "If there's any problem at all right now, it's not yours. I don't owe your father anything'' Still, Peter was beginning to feel more and more like a thief. More than anything, he thought, whether it's good or bad, in my family I seem to function as a catalyst.

He told his mother he was going to take a walk by himself. He didn't want to, but he believed he needed to be alone, to think this thing through. He had to decide if taking up so much of his mother's time made him feel badly out of pity for his father, or if his father's irritation was not important. Maybe Peter needed to be more sharing. Did he really want to be his mother's husband? Is that why he grew up homosexual? Had he wanted to sleep with his grandmother, as well? Is that what psychologists would tell him?

At least the bitter fighting was over in his family. That was what he'd noticed most when he'd come to visit: the quarrels. His parents had been nasty to one another; his sister snubbed him. Often he could stay only a few days before he'd have to go back to the city to relax. It was a battlefield, and now the battle was over, both sides at a draw. The psychological maneuvers were more subtle. Members of the family kept more to themselves, except for Peter's father who had become more dependent, perhaps because he no longer had alcohol as a prop. Vacations in Peter's family could be either good or bad. In order to have a good vacation they would have to forgive one another. There could be no smoldering fires. And Peter, like the other members of his family, still had a few resentments.

Throughout all the years Peter lived in New York, whenever he dreamed of his sister, he was in trouble and his sister would have nothing to do with him. She would never help him; she shut the door in his face. He dreamed of Sara more than he dreamed of his mother and father. He seldom thought about Sara consciously at all, but he'd always been aware of her; her voice spoke constantly in his subconscious. If she just wasn't such a redneck, he thought. If she'd just get out and move to a city and not stay at home for the rest of her life. Education was what she needed.

At the age of fourteen, Peter decided that the pretentious community he was raised in was an unnatural environment. He yearned for a truth in existence that he could not find among the noveau riche. In his silly teens he wanted to know the pains of poverty, of blacks from the south, the desperations in the souls of Forty-Second Street. He subscribed to the *Village Voice* and read the personals. He read Woody Guthrie, and studied, in fact, all the folk heroes of the 1960s.

Sara was interested in sports. She smoked pot, watched television, sometimes rented movies, and owned a car. Peter had other expectations; he was certain that Sara could have been more than that. And Sara had certain expectations of him. She had, for one, expected him to be normal and not homosexual.

One of the reasons that Sara was spoiled by her parents was that they were afraid of her. No one could hold a grudge longer than Sara. If you crossed her in any way, denied her requests, or did not give in to her demands, she would turn you off.

What was Sara's attitude towards Peter's impending death? Did she believe in it? Did she think she could make it go away by putting off all thought of it? What was her attitude? Surely she must have a point of view. Whenever Peter got her close to revealing it, the most she'd ever say would be: "I don't want to talk about it." Even that was a victory, in its way.

When their grandmother had died Sara was made to wear a dress to the funeral. She did it unwillingly, but that was perhaps the last time she ever wore one. She was in just as much of a shock after that ominous phone call as Peter was. But it was Peter who went off the deep end. She only watched their intimate relationship slowly fading. In silent horror she listened one time when he slept overnight in her room. Peter could not contain himself, and after a discussion about their grandmother, he began to cry. It happend once more, three years later, when they were at a relative's on Christmas Eve. The two had shared a bedroom again, shared one as they had when their grandmother was alive and when they spent the weekends with her. Christmas was their grandmother's special day. As Peter and Sara remembered the fun they used to have then, he cried again. He knew that his sister would never again feel at ease about bringing up their grandmother's name. She would always be alone with her own memories. Peter still had too much grief to face his. But today that had changed; Peter *could* talk about his grandmother. For his sister, though, too much time had elapsed for that.

In his imagination, Peter was in the habit of trading years off his life in return for favors from God. For example, to have read *Don Quixote,* or *The Tales of Genji,* Peter would willingly forego three months from the final year of his life. Of course, now he could not spare time in trade. Perhaps dying at twenty-five was a result of a lifetime of too much trading with God. If he knew that he wasn't dying, he'd willingly give a year, so that he and his sister could be intimate again. Since he hadn't kept a record of these transactions, he had no idea how much time he had left before he was overdrawn.

When he returned to the beach house, Peter found that his mother had not yet returned. His father gave him a gruff greeting. Sara was smoking pot and drinking a beer in one of the bedrooms.

"I know this was a mistake," she said when Peter entered.

"You could try a little harder," he told her, sitting down on the bed. His leg itched horribly where he'd applied some of the DNCB lotion to one of his lesions.

She did not like criticism. "Why should I try? Mom and Dad are a little stupid, don't you think?"

"All people are," he said, trying to teach her something, "because life is."

She could ask where he had decided he'd learned so much about life, but she would not. Peter's experiences with people had been homosexual: she did not want to know about them.

"You always have all the answers," she said unpleasantly.

"Do I?" He was genuinely curious. "Is that how it seems to you?"

"You come back here and stir everything up. It happens every time you come home. Everything works, until you arrive."

Peter was horrified. Does she really think this? "But I just want to help things," he said.

"Then stay out of our business."

He could think of nothing to say. He looked out the window at the tall beach grasses bent by the wind, at their sharp yellow tips.

"Some people just like to enjoy themselves," she went on. "You have to dissect everything."

"Am I so wrong?" Peter asked.

"You get on *my* nerves sometimes."

"You betrayed me," he said suddenly. "I'm the one who should be mad. I told you to keep my diary for me once when I'd left it at home, and what did you do? You read it and promptly took it up to Mom's bedroom, and asked her if she knew I was gay. I don't think that was very loyal. You used to be my friend. I could trust you. Now you find it difficult to even look at me."

She said nothing. He started for the door. As he opened it and went out, he looked back with disappointment. He shook his head.

"Why don't you just go back to New York?" she asked.

"And why don't you just die?" he retorted.

"Why don't *you*?" she shouted, loud enough for their father to hear in the next room. "Instead of talking to Mom about it all the time!"

10

As he lay in bed, the sheets damp and clinging to his body, Peter found it easiest not to open his eyes at all. He did not answer anyone when asked a question. He hands shook when his mother offered him a cup of soup broth. Sitting up was an ordeal. In the beginning he had been miserable. He'd ached in every conceivable place; he was cold, no matter how many blankets his mother piled on top of him. Cold water was a relief, but not much. Most of the time he slept. Whole days must have passed. He did not know if he was still at the ocean or at home.

To pass the time he thought. . .

Each decade is marked by something. The 1980s are marked by conservative political aggression and by the epidemic of AIDS. He believed that after 1990 the problems of the eighties would suddenly disappear and people would be faced with a different set. He also believed that his own health would be better: anyone who made it to 1989 would not die of AIDS. It was ridiculous and irrational, but this was what he thought when he was lying there. It all seemed like science fiction to him anyway.

He wished there was a way to read with his eyes closed. Sentences could just appear and there would be absolutely no ocular strain. For hours he could read that way. He wished there was a way you never had to put food into your body: It would just appear there. It would be dispersed to the various parts that needed nutrition. The act of eating struck him as gross; this putting objects into his mouth that went down inside of him. He tucked the ends of the blankets under his feet.

In order to pass the time he tried to remember every Christmas since the age of ten. There had been fourteen since, his fifteenth was only two months away. He had shadowy memories of going to church on Christmas for midnight mass and standing outside with a group of people holding candles. Christmas had always been the pinnacle of the year; it was a ritual with the most mystery behind it, a ceremony when relationships were honored through the giving of presents. So many people had died in Peter's family that Christmas now included only a small number of people — a stray aunt, a cousin.

The recovering health of a person with AIDS is a precarious thing at best. Peter remembered sadly thinking several years before: it's amazing that people can feel so low emotionally and care so little about their fate and yet have nothing bad happen to them. Now he knew how wrong this was. He also remembered that just after feeling so unhappy and disappointed he came down with a severe case of hepatitis B. His doctor said: "You can never drink again." Six months and one million drinks later, disappointed and disillusioned, he had AIDS. I must not permit myself to die, he thought. How will I do this? Every day I must think that I am getting better, that life holds meaning, that there is a point for my being here. And, of course, there *is* one. In order to stay alive each day I must say, "I want to."

His sight was perhaps his biggest problem, one of his eyes especially. When he stared in the mirror he believed he could see the weaker eye slightly out of line with the other. He did know that wall-eyed people disturbed him greatly, and in order to talk to someone with a glass eye he needed to know immediately which one wasn't real so that he could focus on the real eye. This had always been an uneasy situation for him and now he know why: one day that would be his problem. The pupil of one of his eyes would turn further away; perhaps he'd even be, God forbid, wall-eyed like Jean-Paul Sartre.

When old people say they have aches and pains, they mean it. For Peter right now it was his mouth that gave him the most physical discomfort. He had any number of infections inside it. By rolling back his tongue he was able to alleviate some of the discomfort. He'd heard stories of a friend in New York who grew a lesion on his tongue so large that he was unable to eat without pain. It eventually grew so long it stuck out of his mouth. The man's legs had withered. He'd once been a model and a body builder. It was a horror story.

When Peter was diagnosed in the beginning he felt like a diseased monster. Who would want to be close to him now? Yale did, he knew, and this frightened him. The meaning of sex had changed, of course. He couldn't face it. With all the new considerations about AIDS in relation to sex, Peter felt that the pursuit of it, or even the acceptance of it as a natural desire, was impossible. He didn't need to have sex with anyone — ever. This had always been true, except that now he saw clearly that sex, in itself, offered nothing, only heartache. He did not know what he wanted to do with Yale or anyone else. He had no plans, no blueprints for a relationship. He knew his ambivalence would discourage most people. But since he was on uncharted waters anyway, he had no fixed ideas about anything anymore.

The way he felt today, Peter did not want to see Yale. He didn't want to see anyone except his family, and even then he had reservations about Sara and his father. There was no answer, except to let go, to let go of everything, to let things simply take their course. But he did have feelings towards Yale that he could not deny. It was up to time to provide answers.

The change in Peter's attitude towards sex was not entirely bad. In the past he'd wanted to reach this point, where sex was not a controlling factor in his life. Now it wasn't, but not for entirely "good" reasons. Still, he saw the truth of his position. His only goal now was to get better, to stop being sick, and to apply his new knowledge to being alive.

Peter lay in bed very still. He knew that he was at home in the caretakers cottage and that it was cold. In the mornings it was completely white outside from the fog. He could only see a hundred feet from the window. He could not make out the lake. An hour before the white fog came, there was a blue mist and the lights of the boat docks would still be lit.

People came and went. It was not important anymore who they were; it was only important that hands touched him, brought him things. He did not associate the hands with faces.

When he was much younger and unable to sleep at night, he had been able to recount every experience he could remember from the very first. He was able to call them up chronologically. When he had come to the present he was so tired and hollow inside that he would be able to sleep, usually only a few hours before dawn. He didn't know if he had the strength to do this today. He was also fairly certain that over the past five years a good many of his memories had, through disuse, fallen away.

He thought of a wallet he used to carry in high school. In it he kept a snapshot of his grandmother. Where most men carried photographs of girlfriends, this was what he carried. He knew it was odd, and for this reason and several others he got into the habit of seldom revealing himself. But now he had neither wallet nor photographs to hide. He'd never had a wallet in New York: his money just balled up in his pockets. He never had it for more than a day or two anyway, before he needed a fresh supply. Most of his money had been spent at night.

* * *

He was burning up. The only relief was sleep. He wanted to leave his body. He didn't want arms or legs.

"Can I get anything for you?"

He didn't answer.

"I think he's very sick. Should we call a doctor?"

Peter listened to all of this. They don't think I can hear them, he thought. I understand everything. But then he would fall away again and drown in sleep.

Certain voices he liked better than others. There was one moment when he woke up to a thumping in his ears. He thought someone had entered the bedroom and was rustling a sheet loudly next to his bed. He was terrified. Then he realized it was the sound of his heart. Gradually the noise stopped.

His shoulders hurt. His legs hurt.

A massage would be the answer to much of the problem, but he did not know whom to ask. He'd made Yale promise to call him daily, but since Peter had gone on vacation to the oceanside, he had not notified Yale of his return. Now he didn't want to, not in the state he was in. Of course, he was aware that this was not right; the whole purpose of their friendship was to nurture. Should one of them ever get sick, the other would not forget; neither would be cut off from all social contact and drown in the heart of the family. But Peter was too weak to talk now. Until he was better he could think of nothing to say to anyone.

Long before he knew or suspected that he was going to die, he thought about his great-grandmother's sister, Aunt Neoma, or "Oma," as she was called. Oma had died of tuberculosis at the age of twenty, aggravated, they said, by a broken heart. While both her older sisters had married and settled down to families, young Neoma had gone to Portland to make her way as a seamstress. She was tempermental and artistic.

In the homes of relatives, Peter still saw traces of her talents: a book of drawings in one attic, a red rose embroidered on a cloth hanging in a bedroom, a handpainted thimble in a brass box, the engraved pen set from the man who jilted her on a cousin's mantel. There was also a letter from her that Peter had found tied up in silk among his great-grandparents' love letters. Although he was weak now, Peter fished in the drawer by his bed and found his red leather folder. Without moving his head or eyes, he felt for the brittle paper, and locating it, he pulled it out. The letter was addressed to one of Neoma's in-laws, a politican and justice of the peace. The return address was the Martha Washington Hotel for Women. He read the familiar letter again:

My dear friend:

No, I have not gone back to Portland, nor changed my name. I had expected to go back but a sudden turn in the wheel of fate changed my plans, as it did my whole life, in fact. I will tell you my trouble and ask your judgment of my course of action. Shortly after I became engaged, I noticed a trait in the character of my fiance that I did not understand, and which was exceedingly repulsive to me. I decided to put him to the test to see if he could be true to me when I was away from him. So I came home. I was not anxious to pledge my life to him unless he could be sincere and true. Everything went all right – his letters came regularly, twice a week, with news of how he was fixing a home for me. Just a month ago, however, a letter came later than usual, telling me point-blank that he was afraid if he married me he could not be true to me, and he would rather not marry at all. It was as if someone had stabbed me. But after consideration I see it is all for the best. God was good. I was saved from a life of misery, for it would have been so if I had married him. It hurts one so to see an ideal fall apart, but I killed all my love for him when I realized he was untrue and not worthy of me. It is hard to do and I know I must do it. But it has destroyed my faith in humanity, with a few exceptions, of course. He did not ask me to answer so I have not written, or heard from him again. I should not have burdened you with this, but I have to be gay and not tell the folks how I care. But I felt that I must tell you. I wish I could see you and talk to you. I guess I will have to come down and look after you, see that you get your train, etc. I am feeling pretty good now, but I have suffered with a heavy cold on my lungs and an attack of indigestion, and severe mental strain that has kept me down for a few days. But I am all right now, with the exception of my cold, which will persist in staying with me. Well, my dear, I must bring this letter to a close. I thank you from the depths of my heart for your regard for me. It does me a world of good to know there is someone who cares for me and is interested in my welfare. I trust this finds you well. With sincerest regards for you, I am always your affectionate little girl.

Neoma

Peter knew she died of TB a month after the letter was written. The year was 1906 and in one of her brother-in-law's letters Peter remembered reading: "I wish I could do something for Oma, but I guess no one can help her now."

In the drawer of his nightstand he also kept a book that he knew Neoma had been reading shortly before her death. It was Oliver Wendell Holmes' *The Autocrat of the Breakfast-Table*. He opened it and read at random:

"Mark this which I am going to say, for it is as good as a working professional man's advice, and costs you

*nothing: It is better to lose a pint of blood from your
veins than to have a nerve tapped."*

What's that supposed to mean? he wondered impatiently. He flipped through more pages:

*"I remember a young wife who had to part with
her husband for a time. She did not write a mourn-
ful poem; indeed, she was a silent person, and perhaps
hardly said a word about it; but she quietly turned
of a deep orange color with jaundice. A great many
people in this world have but one form of rhetoric
for their profoundest experiences, namely, to waste
away and die."*

Wading through a hundred sermons and observations, he
finally came upon:

*"I go for the man who inherits family traditions
and the cumulative humanities of at least four or five
generations."*

Day-dreaming, he wished briefly that he could write letters
and send them backwards in time. He wished his Aunt Neoma
could answer them from her viewpoint while still on earth.

In the middle of the book he found an old photo of the
Portland Women's Union, made up of four members: Neoma,
her sister, and two friends. Neoma was playing a guitar and
her sister, a violin, an instrument that nearly all of Peter's family
had learned to play, except for his own father who as a boy
was taught to play the harp. There was even a photograph to
prove it.

"You are tempermental like Aunt Neoma," his grandmother had once told Peter. "You are sensitive, as she was."

Although he didn't understand how, Peter knew even then
that he was being complimented. Now he laughed. Grandma, he thought, you were so right. Both Neoma and I will
have died young and for roughly the same reason —
disillusionment. It seemed to Peter as if his experiences in
the world, with romance and with other people had led him

to this end. He was no different from Neoma. He put the book and letter away.

He could feel his throat. It was hot. The lesion on his tongue irritated him. It felt swollen against his teeth. He had indigestion, too, and the pain in his stomach, he suspected, came as a result of all the vitamins he was taking. His jaw ached; his hands shook uncontrollably. Gradually he was becoming weaker.

11

As Peter's fever rose he dreamed. A verse came back to him from his teenage years: "He remembered the death of his grandmother. In childhood's spectrum of violence, she remained pure."

He dreamed about the village where his grandmother was raised. They were living in one of the great old Victorian farm houses with trees and valleys spread out before them – a gray road, like a ribbon, going off into the distance. It was winter in Oregon farm country.

Peter's entire family was now present at the dining table, his grandma at the head. As they celebrated her return from the hospital, all at once her head fell off. Black liquid came oozing out.

"You'll never be the same once you quit drugs and alcohol. You'll be boring and you won't be any fun. You might even die more quickly by giving them up. People have heart attacks when they stop drinking. AIDS sets in after people mend their ways."

Peter squeezed through the opening in the gate. Suddenly he was closed in by trees and a low flint wall. Here a creek ran down through timber and watercress. It was very quiet and still with only the sounds of an owl and the water. A barely perceptible carriage track was cut into the grass. He followed it through the tangled undergrowth. His grandmother's white house loomed up through the trees. He could see the flock of sheep that lived in the house at night, grazing in the thicket by the farm's out buildings.

"You are only recuperating so that you can go back and get completely bombed for the rest of your life, however long that may be."

Coming into the grape arbor, he went through the little gate, past the sheds. He went into the springhouse that straddled the creek and washed his face there in the chilly water of the rock pool. Crossing the old flower garden, kept irrigated all these years by the creek, he came to the back porch of his grandma's house. Instead of entering, he went around toward the cider mill and past the smokeshed.

"Why were you so hell-bent on destroying yourself, when the very thought of dying of AIDS terrified you?"

Standing in the pasture, near the large stand of pampas grass, with the enormous shadows passing over, Peter looked fixedly at the house. The doors on the porch were gone and the windows broken, but sweet peas and scarlet runner still grew on the pillars. After making his way through the sagging ivy trellis, he went inside. In the musty hallway he ran his fingers along the texture of the wallpaper.

"Watch Peter. Watch him burn. The ball is rolling. How long will the show last? It was already too late. It was too late a long time ago. Laugh, Peter, there's only one other choice."

As he came up the familiar lane, the fields below looked like a yellow sea. When he passed the knoll where the church stood blazing white in the shade, a wind was rustling the branches of an oak tree. He looked up at the sky.

"You have had an alcohol and drug problem."

He came bicycling up the narrow dusty road that led through the countryside. The wide dale of green lawns bottomed out below him, and the knoll rose up more and more clearly in the sun. He could see a ridge of pale blue trees. To the left were the purple hills of Grass Valley, Shaniko, and Bakeoven. As he turned the bend, the little church ahead glowed white against them.

Peter fell from his bicycle.

Brittle golden leaves blew about him and his bare legs felt damp against the cold grass. He ran his fingers lightly across the hairs of his leg; they looked like golden grass in a field. There was a patch of sun coming through the roof of trees onto the floor of the hillside. He rolled over so that the brightness was not in his eyes.

"You got over your fear of needles quickly, Peter. What are you going to do now? Fill your veins again and be content? Fill up with the Atlantic ocean? BAM. Suddenly everything feels so differrent. It's time to float, Peter. Tomorrow never comes. People can smell the drugs coming out of your pores."

Someone is just going to have to tell your grandmother."

It was raining and he was shaking. He turned over and lay down, his hands folded under his chest. A vein of lightning flashed brightly. It was dusk now, the sky orange. He hoped the raccoons would come out, their eyes shining yellow like a cat's. A great roar of wind was coming up through the tall fir trees. The rain was falling hard and steady on the leak roof. He clambered down the mossy stairs and took off on his bicycle into the cool rain. For a long distance, he could see the spire of Zena church sticking up crooked in the gray sky.

"Dead people can see you, Peter. Your grandmother is watching you. She always was, and you've been aware of it, too. This enabled you to be proud at moments, and understandably ashamed at others. When a relative died you thought that person would take messages to heaven. But sometimes your grandmother could see for herself. She could see the things you never told anyone."

On the sixth day Peter's fever seemed to decrease. He was able to recognize voices and he could feel the icy cold of a doctor's stethoscope on the cleft of his chest, a blood pressure pad squeezing his arm.

"I dreamed that God was talking to me and that I visited Zena, the place where grandma was born," he said to whoever was in the room.

But then he drifted off again.

"Your mother is in your room, going through it, looking for details. She is looking for clues to find out who you really are."

The voices came back, but Peter's visions had lessened in potency. He was no longer in the country. The landscapes were different now, the topography a conglomeration of all the cityscapes he'd ever known. It was a city of his own creation.

"Do you want to become an alcoholic, like your father?

Then don't go back to New York. Why do you think you got so sick in the first place?"

There were two apple trees and one day they would be large. Peter and his grandmother had planted them on her "lot" near the golfcourse. When they came to water them each evening after dinner, Peter would cut down some of the Canadian thistle to make way for a garden. There was one particularly large thistle that grew against the lamp post on the corner. With a sharp object he measured the stock every few weeks and wrote the date on the post. Even then he felt the need to preserve; he sensed that life could change irrevocably.

When his grandmother was dead he came back that September to pick the tomatoes. There weren't very many; he wasn't surprised. He'd learned to accept disappointment. Perhaps neighbors had stolen them.

Although his mother had sold the lot several years ago and a house had been built over their garden, Peter still, in his imagination, could see their lot as it was. He could also imagine the house that his grandmother would have built for them. It would have been in the Roman style with the windows facing an inner courtyard.

"Grandma, can I have a loft in my bedroom?"
"You sure can. We can make it however you want."

Peter's throat was parched. It was so dry that when he swallowed it tickled and he coughed.

When he opened his eyes he couldn't remember where he was. He could see Sara dancing animatedly on a lawn, ducking the water from the sprinkler system that piped water from the lake to the backyard. She was ten years old, the age when he loved her most. Sara was a sweet girl. He loved her.

* * *

Peter woke, tears streaming down his face. He pulled the blankets up over his head and dreamed about a particular spot in the trees behind his parents' old house where he had grown up. Immediately after his grandmother died, he'd sat there on the pine-needle floor and didn't know what to do with himself. He brought his sister there once, and they buried a bird in a silver music box they improvised as a coffin.

From that spot in the trees he could see the road, the house, the lawns, and the bamboo garden. Memories came to him quickly, flashing like lightning. Shame. Humiliation. Anger. Love. Is this what is meant by life that passes before one's eyes upon death?

His visions became more and more chaotic. Even with great effort he could not conjure up his grandmother's birthplace, the narrow backroads, the old schoolhouse, the spring where gypsies had camped and where babies were stolen. All he could see was rain. It was raining on the lake.

"Just look, it's raining pitchforks and black babies."
now the voice of his great-grandmother from Kansas.
He woke. He was icy cold.

When his friend wasn't looking Peter threw a stone at the church's window. It shattered. "Why didn't you tell me you were going to do that? I would have thrown one, too."

From their lookout point in the trees Peter and his school friend could see the cars from the grade school. They collected the rotting apples from the orchard and made a stack of them. When a car passed Peter and his friend would throw an apple. Peter always threw the hardest.

"My son can no longer spend the afternoons with Peter. It's not that Peter is a bad boy, it's just that together they bring out the rebel in each other." It wasn't the first time a mother had said it.

Pyromania: "The uncontrollable impulse to start fires." Peter liked to watch things burn as a kid — dolls disfigured, toy cars melted.

"Your grandmother died because you were bad."

"But I'm not bad. I'm just sensitive. My puberty was more violent. I was trying to deal with the pressures my father's alcoholism was having on me."

"An excuse."

In the forest across the street from where Peter grew up there was a log. On that log Peter and a friend had smoked their first cigarettes and gotten dizzy and sick. Drugs came years later. In that forest he had seen a neighbor boy running naked. Things happened in these woods. Teenagers drank beer, girls got pregnant.

"A drug addict, alcoholic, deceitful sexual pervert, dying of a disease of the morals. Who would have thought it then, yet clearly the path had been marked." The voice in Peter's head was speaking again.

"Oh, shut up," he told it.

"You broke your mother's heart."
"Stop it."

The fever continued to pulsate through him. He no longer tried to fight it or the thoughts that passed through his mind. The dark lids of his eyes were movie screens. He let go. . . .

"What about the sterling your mother claimed you stole

from her and sold to satisfy a drug urge, to go to bars and meet your kind of people?"

"The silver belonged to someone my mother hated."

"She felt you betrayed her. You were showing her your utter contempt for the sanctity of family life."

"What good is all this? It isn't true."

"That afternoon when you daydreamed that your grandmother died in a car accident? Do you remember? Your evil thoughts are what made her die a month later."

"But I thought that was God preparing me for her death."

"It wasn't."

In the darkness Peter, as a child, believed he could see faces in the patterns of the tree branches. From his window the trees stood out, long tree trunks that shot up into the sky, taller than skyscrapers. Some day, he thought, one of them would fall.

In the attic of the house where he was born there was an altar with a brass face.

"You were too young to remember the house in Laurelhurst."

"Then what was I remembering?"

From the big windows that faced the forest, people could easily see inside. "There's a man out there," one night Peter shouted.

"Peter sees things that don't exist."

The fever shifted about like ice glaciers moving inside him. Gradually he came out of it. He was more and more aware of the room he lay in. He was able to confirm that it was daylight, that the sun had come out, that it was his mother who was speaking to him.

12

There was a blue fog over the lake. Two small yellow lights shone from the other bank. It had stopped raining at daybreak, but there was still a steady flow of water from the drain pipes down to the pavement on the patio. The windows of the caretaker's cottage were cold and damp. It was the first rainy day in November and the farmers of Oregon, the firefighters, and the citizens of Portland who had no water in their public drinking fountains would be glad for the rain. It had been a very dry fall.

Peter sat up in bed. He was too cold to move any further. Instead he stared out the windows, his eyes never shifting. He stared at the sky through an opening in the trees. His mother was holding his hand. She pulled the afghan, one her mother had knit, closer to Peter's chin.

"You kept talking in your sleep," she said as he looked at her.

Beside his bed there were white carnations, the edges trimmed in red. When he leaned close to smell them his first thought was that they reminded him of his father who, as an usher in church, wore a carnation every Sunday when Peter was a boy. Carnations reminded him of the bottled milk delivered every morning from the Carnation Dairy.

"What was I talking about?" he asked.

"My mother." She put a thermometer in his mouth. "You

were talking about your grandmother. You still think of her, don't you?''

He nodded and pushed the thermometer further under his tongue.

"I don't think of her everyday anymore," she continued. "It was twelve years ago. I miss her the most when I'm tired, because I could always drive up to her house when I couldn't face the world anymore. When I was tired of being a mother and a wife, she'd take you and Sara for awhile. I miss doing things with her like going shopping. She was there when I grew up, when I was sick. She represented security to me. Now when I get very tired I dream only of climbing into a cave and sealing it off with a rock, where nothing can touch me.''

He took the thermometer out and read: 102. "When you lose someone you love," he said, speaking from some mysterious experience, "you age five years at least. It's guaranteed." He closed his eyes. When you die, he thought, before the white light takes you away, they say that for several moments you float above your body, which you can see lying below you. He wondered what it would be like to die in an airplane, to float without a body momentarily in the clouds. What visual perspective did the members of *Space Challenger* have when their rocket exploded, or the riders of the *Hindenberg* when it went up in flames? In the ocean, would the spirit float to the surface or would it glide about through the mouth of a shark?

When his mother went up to the big house to get him some soup, Peter sat up. He saw his mother's knitting chair. Next to it was a folder of newspaper clippings. She had just cut out a new article. He looked at it: "Preliminary data from a study of 843 men in San Francisco indicate that personal attitude and the amount of social support received can affect how well the immune system functions. Certain conditions significantly affect the number of some subjects' T-cells, one of the more important indicators of immune system functioning." Peter pushed the folder and the clipping aside. People with AIDS can wish their life away, he thought.

Whom do you like better? Me or Sara? Peter could remember asking this of his mother quite often as a child. It was important that Peter learn how to stand up without anyone else's assistance. The only way to be proud is to be proud of one's self. But AIDS — disease and illness — is somehow wrapped up in all of this. You get AIDS from close physical contact, but it is also a spiritual disease. In order to overcome it you have to become healthy and happy, however that is possible, not feel as if you are being punished or that society does not accept you. This pressure alone is enough to give anyone a deadly disease. At home now he must not be concerned with rejections from boyhood friends, from family members.

"What is his threshold of pain?" a doctor had asked once when Peter was lying moaning in a hospital bed. None of his friends present could answer. "We're not really sure if he's strong or not." If I really am strong, he thought, I'm definitely getting less so.

Before Peter had gotten so sick at the oceanside, he'd spoken to Yale on the telephone. The conversation came back to him now full force. He'd been struck by Yale's willingness to give in. Yale had said that he wanted to go back to wherever he'd come from, that he'd completed his mission, that his life had been an experiment, the tests completed and over. "The purpose of life," Yale had continued, "is only to experience. Once you've experienced life to its fullest, for what you deem to be a long enough time and up until the time your body gives out, all you have to do is feel it and see it for what it is."

Human life, Peter knew, was often lived badly, and stupidly, but he believed that people lived it the best they could. A lot of pain could be avoided, he thought, but Yale's argument was that pain didn't need to be avoided. "Why should

it?'' he'd said. "Do what you have to do and then get out.
And try to take your stain with you. You don't owe life
anything.'' But Peter had not found Yale's words easy to accept. He wanted to believe that there was more to
accomplish in life than just to live it. What had happened to
Yale that had suddenly made him change so violently?

"Open as many doors as you'd like," Yale had said, "stay
in some rooms longer than in others, see every floor, and then
get out. There's nothing dignified about living to be ninety
years old.''

But Peter disagreed. He thought old people could be an
inspiration — that is, old people who could still function and
be happy. When Peter asked him, Yale said that he was not
mad at God for AIDS. "AIDS," he explained, "is what you get
when you live as we did. You can't walk across that many
hot coals and not get burned. At a certain point you start
repeating the major discoveries about people, and their relationships to the exterior world. Then it comes time to settle
back in and apply your wisdom. . .and die.''

Peter had found all this a bit incomplete. There *had* to
be more to life. Yale went on to tell him that the only tragedy
in life, as he saw it, was being denied the mental capacity to
see truth always. "What is truth?'' Peter had asked. "That
nothing in this world matters," Yale had answered. "If you
can keep this perception long enough you will die. In order
to stay warmly inside your body you must be enchanted with
mundanity. To have to be confined in a body in the first place
is petty. It's like William James said, maybe we're all just
parasites on some huge animal, we're all inside some enormous organism that we can't see. There is nothing noble about
human life. Joy has no more value than despair; hunger is
worse. Life is here to be seen and felt. Do as much of both
as possible, then get out. Worrying is the worst thing life has
to offer. To worry is to obsess, to obsess is to limit perception, but not to worry is impossible. The most dignified thing

I can do now is die – the plane has started to land, don't circle around the airport, just bring it in."

Peter felt that there needed to be more of a fight. Life was all about fighting. You couldn't give in to it. He remembered a man standing in a bar one time, bleary-eyed from days of drugs, who'd said, "it's so hard to distinguish between reality and fantasy." People had laughed. But not Peter. To think you see something was to see it. He remembered being certain one summer that the police were going to come to his door that day and arrest him. Of course, logically, he knew there was no reason to think this, but he sat back and waited anxiously for them to knock. He didn't think that there had to be a particular reason. He was very tired when this happened. His hotel room was only a rock under which he hid each day. Anything could happen; the worse often did. Reality/fantasy/reality/fantasy — which is which? When he panicked on the street he kept walking until he dropped. Actual death, Peter thought, could be very anticlimatic. It was good to know when, how, where, and why you were going to die. To have a sudden death was to be robbed of the sensation that nothing in life mattered, as Yale had pointed out. But to be too long about death was op- pressive. Perhaps that was what Yale was trying to say.

"Can I please go now?" Yale had jokingly asked. "The only life to regret is one that is not lived, one that has not been experimented with, one that has been too complacent." But wasn't fighting death a valid experience? He would have to ask Yale this question once he saw him. Since his high fever, Peter had not had an opportunity.

About his own death: when the music started, for himself, he wanted to have a glorious fall — a drug and alcohol weekend. He wanted to push it all the way, and then fall into the arms of God.

When his mother came back into the room he was tired. He couldn't think of anything to say.

"Would you like me to spend the day with you on Saturday? If you feel better we could go to a gallery. Perhaps the
Pittock Mansion?"

Peter thought: that's five days from now. I must get out
on my own and do something. I must see Yale and get some
things straight. He explained this to his mother and she looked annoyed.

"Do you plan to spend the entire day with him?"

He looked at her. He couldn't always read his mother.
He knew that in the past he felt a lot of guilt in relation to
her but nothing was tangible enough to talk about. His
mother distrusted everyone; she feared that all her children
wanted was to drink and get high on drugs. He knew she
feared that terrible forces could take hold of her two children.
When Peter was away in New York and she didn't see him,
she didn't worry as much. He did not ask her for money, and
she did not have to feel that she was contributing to any
debaucheries. She feared that they went on behind her back,
and to a certain degree she was right. But in his mind Peter
believed that the bad things that happened to him had less
to do with drugs or alcohol than simply with his difficulty
being in his body; it was something more existential. He
wanted to be able to talk about the good and bad things that
happened to him in the world. But, if he was not doing alcohol
or drugs his mother could offer only sympathy; her answer
was simply not to live in the world, to stay home instead.
His blood and her blood were the same, but his blood had
been poisoned by going out into the world. If he had stayed
at home she could have offered him a safe haven. But if Peter
did not die right away, could he live in a protective and yet
stale environment without anything good or bad happening
to him? He needed to go on with his project — his interac-
tions with other people, the development of his self-
confidence, the furthering of the ball already set into motion.
AIDS was not the culmination. Some kind of successful end

was needed. Was it that he was alive after all that had happened?

"Your father is sitting up at the house, waiting."

"Why don't you spend the day with him on Saturday?"

"I suppose I could," she said without interest.

"Mom", he asked, "do you really want me to stay home with you?"

Her eyes became cloudy. "I want you to have fun," she said. "I know it's boring here with us. But I can't stop being your mother, and I worry that you won't eat or get enough rest if you go into town. You can't blame me, Peter. I don't want you not to have fun, I want you to go and be with people your own age while you can."

"I'd feel better, too, if you spent more time with Dad," he said.

"The last time I didn't spend much of the weekend at home, your father marched outside in the cold and stood on the back porch. It was so funny I felt sorry for him, as I would for a child. I agreed not to go into town that night without him, even though he hates to be with any of my friends."

Peter did need to get out more and be with people his own age. Thinking about it triggered some of his feelings of guilt for not attending the national March on Washington several weeks before. He should have gone. He told this to his mother.

"I'm very glad you didn't." she responded. "What good would that have done? It seems to me your energies could have been better spent just by taking care of yourself, by staying alive, which isn't always the easiest thing for a person with AIDS to do. What would be the point of marching anyway? Everyone knows about AIDS by now, don't they? I even see it on daytime soap operas."

"The reason for the demonstration," he explained, a little disturbed, "was for legal recognition of gay relationships, a Presidential order banning discrimination by the federal government, the repeal of all laws discriminating on the basis of sexual orientation, and an end to discrimination against people with AIDS. There were plenty of reasons, and we had as many arrests at that demonstration as they did during the Vietnam ones."

His mother wiped a warm towel across his forehead. "Lie back and relax," she said.

But more than anything he just wanted to get out of bed. He was weary of being sick. The fever he felt now was to be outside, to be in Portland, to be talking to Yale. He closed his eyes and remembered all of the azalea bushes his mother once had – red, yellow, pink. In the spring, as a child, he would snap off the blossoms . . . and arrange them into words on the lawn. Suddenly he wanted to do this, he wanted to go outside, snap off flower blossoms and write his name with them. But it was fall now, turning into winter – the leaves were orange and yellow, and in several weeks snow would start to fall.

"I wrote you a poem," his mother said. She read it to him out loud: "Tall and stately fir, what makes you stand so straight? Tall and stately fir, what makes your branches sway? Is it the wind that touches you? Or is it God you try to reach?"

13

Yesterday," Yale, said, looking up at Peter from a mound
of blankets, "I thought I saw more lesions on my arm. But
I didn't look very carefully because I didn't care. It's not that
I hate myself today, if I hate anything it's this world, not life —
life and the world are two different things. Life itself is
precious."

Peter felt chilly in Yale's studio. The heater was on, but
outside they both could see that it was a gray day and fall was
definitely coming to an end. There was a draft in the room.

"All I know is," Yale continued, "I just want to go home,
and I can't seem to because there is no such thing as home
anymore. I'm not going to lie to you, Peter. You'll understand
that I'm not fighting anymore."

Peter breathed deeply. No, he wasn't making any
judgments.

"You can take it to mean I'm giving in," Yale went on
from his bed, "but that doesn't mean that I won't keep sup-
porting your life if you want to live through this. I'll keep on
telling you all the information I can about medications."

In spite of Yale's reassurances, Peter felt deserted.

"I want you to know about meditation, too, Peter. It's
very important in reducing your anxiety level. All of us who
have AIDS know that any anxiety can be very harmful. I was
studying Buddhism techniques here in Portland at the Vedanta
Society, and it helped me for awhile. I was leary of the religious

aspect, but I think you will find that you only have to accept as much as you want. It's the meditation, the clearing of the mind that's so important. And if it's true that God resides in us, then maybe it can be easier to contact him, to tap the source of that power to heal ourselves of AIDS. I want you to pursue it, Peter, and if I wasn't in bed right now I would take you to a meeting myself. I've written down the address and their phone number. Will you call them?"

Peter nodded. On the hot plate the water was boiling. He turned it off and poured them both cups of hot chocolate. Yale had a difficult time sitting up.

"What I don't understand," Peter said, taking his seat again, "is why you're giving up. Although I realize if I was five years older I might not fight either."

"The gay scene has really changed," Yale explained. "People have stopped experimenting. I was supposed to be some kind of messenger, that's all. My purpose has been spent. All I know is that I just want to go home. We took our life-style as far as we could."

"Have you lost interest in everything?" Peter asked.

"I suppose I have. I haven't lost my interest in individuals, just in the world. You still interest me."

Peter sighed, "I brought you a book," he said. "It just came out." He read to Yale from the dust jacket: "Shilts traces the untold story of medical mysteries and human tragedies, scientific intrigue and sexual politics, astonishing courage and petty deceit. He shows that the epidemic spread wildly because the federal government put budget ahead of the nation's welfare; health authorities placed political expediency before the public health; and scientists were often more concerned with international prestige than saving lives." He handed the thick tome to Yale.

Yale took it. "I think even if I did have my health back I'd be very disoriented," he began. "Because the gay world seems to have gone in a very different direction. I'm like the last remaining guest at a party; everyone has gone home but I'm not ready to. 'Last Call.' It's fear. I wasn't prepared for the conservative eighties. My friends all belonged to a different period."

"Mine, too," Peter said. "Maybe that's why we became friends. We sensed a similarity, a certain hostility towards the present, that perhaps we knew and belonged to a period that was superior." Peter smiled. "Do you remember when people were saying that AIDS was really King Tut's curse? It came with his remains when they went on exhibition here in 1976."

Yale frowned. "I love life, you know," he said, ignoring Peter's remark. "I know people wouldn't understand this, but I love it now because time is precious and also because there isn't much of it left. I want to leave on good terms. I don't want to hate it. I don't have to hate it to want to leave it, do I?"

"I don't know." Peter said. He felt confused.

"Each of us has a different internal clock," Yale continued. "Maybe it's not necessary for me to live to be old to do what I have to."

"No, it's not necessary," Peter echoed. "I'd just like a good solid five more years myself, that's all. I'd like to live to thirty."

"Well, I have two years until then," Yale told him. "I wonder if I'll make it."

It was true that Yale looked awful, like a man who had gone without sleeping for several days and has seen a ghost on top of it. He was thinner, but so was Peter. Peter's hands seemed to shake more than Yale's did, however, although Peter was out of bed and Yale was not. Their skin looked pasty and Peter was only comfortable outdoors wearing sunglasses.

The problem for Yale, he explained, was that life in itself was not rewarding enough. He was grateful for good health when he had it, but like Peter he had to have another reason to continue. Life was only something to be gotten through as easily as possible, with as much satisfaction as could be found.

Gay life once held the promise of much more than Yale found
it offered now. Somebody, somewhere had exaggerated its
potentials and rewards. People were cutthroats, and Yale knew
he was responsible for his own experiences with other men.
He told this to Peter. He said that he had to blame himself
as much as he did anyone else. "But once you blame yourself
for your problems, then what do you do?"

Peter shook his head.

"Whatever I do wrong, it's my own fault," Yale told him.
"Life's offerings in gay society have boundaries. We were born
into this situation and the most we can hope for as young gays
is to be able to work with these conditions. But your life, Peter,
should have fewer causes for disillusionment – you're younger.
You'll get to see the right-wing Republicans of the eighties fall
on their knees in the nineties."

Peter could think of nothing to say.

"What was I born for exactly?" Yale asked. "Was it
really only to die of AIDS? To know this one experience?
If it was for anything else, have I failed at accomplishing it,
whatever it was? Could it be enough to have met you, to give
you information on drugs, on medication? If our only purpose in life is to help each other, why should my life be more
important than yours?" He closed he eyes to rest.

"Perhaps the only reason that you'll live longer than me,"
Yale continued, "has to do with the fact that I got sick before
you and before many drugs for treating AIDS were available.
My immune system is more damaged. The best thing I can
offer with my life is to trade off whatever my purpose has
been and give what information I can to you, so that you can
carry on. The best thing a person with AIDS can hope for
is to upset the least number of people as possible. You have
more of a family than I do. That is the most important thing.
Suffering never helped anyone. My parents are dead; no one
will really mourn me."

"But is my mother's pain, for example, the ultimate

horror?" Peter asked. "Can't your life be more important than other people's sorrow? It's got to mean more than that."

"It doesn't have to mean more than bringing people sorrow. Besides my brother, who is coming out here next week, my death won't really hurt anyone else."

"I don't understand this," Peter said, beginning to shake more.

"If I could," Yale went on, "I would gradually exchange my life for someone else's, if only it were that simple. If only I could be a stepping stone somehow for someone else's destiny. AIDS teaches humility. It teaches narcissistic people that their existence is irrelevant."

"Are you tired?" Peter asked. "Would you like me to go?"

With his eyes closed, Yale shook his head. "I will continue to fight" he said, "but the fight is no longer for me. As a human being I have an obligation to fight an oppressor, but I can only do it with another objective in mind. I love you, Peter. I don't ever have to sleep with you to prove it. Sex never made anything more real, it never made love more real. Look at our gay society. Does touching someone really magnify honest feelings? With all my heart I pray that you'll live."

Peter was perspiring.

"Who was the last person you were intimate with?" Yale asked him.

"A young man named Tom I met in a bar." Peter answered calmly. "I told him I was unsure of how I felt about sex and didn't want to do it even with another person who had AIDS. But he wanted me to come over to his house anyway to use his jacuzzi. He told me that he had been diagnosed with AIDS, too, so he understood some of my feelings. He said that he and his lover were so open that sometimes they even had sex with three or four people together. He told me his lover would feel comfortable with whatever happened. So I went with Tom and met his lover. But when his lover heard I had AIDS he

got out of the jacuzzi. I was really hurt. I also didn't understand why Tom's lover was afraid of me, when Tom had told
me he had AIDS, too. Then I understood that either his lover
of a year and a half knew nothing about it, or that Tom had
lied just to get me to have sex with him. When the lover found
us holding each other he asked us both to leave. Tom and his
lover argued, and then neither would speak to me. It was the
very thing I tried to explain to Tom, when I met him and
agreed to go with him. I was afraid that having sex had become
too complicated, it wasn't a simple thing anymore, that didn't
take responsibility. Tom's lover kicked him out right there. And
Tom lost his home, all because he was with someone who
had AIDS. I was the bad guy.''

Yale reached over and grasped Peter's knee. "I'm glad we
never had sex," he said. "We didn't need to, did we?''

"It wasn't necessary," Peter answered. "But one of my
favorite people once said, 'I try to allow myself sexual gratifica-
tion whenever I am attracted to someone who I know is
trustworthy.' Maybe I still feel that way, but that's just it —
no one seems trustworthy enough now, or maybe that just
isn't true anymore. Who can be sure of what anyone really
feels?''

"There's one thing I like about living in Portland," Yale
said. "Life isn't quite as threatening. It always was on the East
Coast, which made me a lot smarter, but it didn't make me
a better person. I think I can die with dignity in Portland. I
think if the gay people here knew I was sick they'd be concerned, not repelled.''

"In some places I know it's like being a senior citizen,"
Peter said. "That's how I felt in San Francisco. Somebody I
trusted spread the word that I had AIDS in all of the bars I
frequented. The bartenders would often frown at me when
I would get high, some people said awful things. I'd never
been treated like that before, and I wasn't ready for it.''

"If the people in Portland do drugs at all in 1987," Yale

said, "it's not something they have to hid. You're not looked down on socially. There's less contact with the police. I think in general life has been better here than anywhere else."

It was true, Peter felt, that a person could live gracefully in Portland. "San Francisco is the epitome of everything that's wrong with gay life," he said.

"At least in Portland we're not living on top of the San Andreas fault line," Yale said. "Life here doesn't shake you up so badly."

"They still have drag queens here," Peter added, "and they aren't as mean. And people listen to what you have to say. I vote for living here and I hope our community stays very small. Let all those vicious big city gays stay together."

"I agree," Yale said, "except that I'm not even really a part of the gay community anymore. I just have my AIDS meetings — that's it. I stopped reading the newspapers; I couldn't read anymore about AIDS. The gays who live in New York, San Francisco, and Los Angeles have their story, but in small towns we also have ours. I think we're easier on each other. I think we're easier on ourselves. I'm glad I gave up the city."

"I'm still fluctuating," Peter said. "Sometimes I have insomnia on Saturday nights."

"To me," Yale said, "San Francisco, more than anywhere, was only a place where I lived and was given constant information. I don't think I ever even stopped and thought about whether I was having a good day. Instead it was always: How many people did I meet? What did I accomplish? And in the end, what did I really accomplish anyway? I got AIDS. Which city do you blame for yours?"

"San Francisco," Peter said, playing along, "without question."

"Me, too," Yale agreed.

"When I left New York," Peter said, "I came to Portland and went downtown to this bar called Flossie's. It's open all

the time, and at night it has orange lights and serves food.
The crowd is a little underworldly — it's like a European all-
night cafe."

"I know the one," Yale said. "The bathhouse upstairs?"

"That's it. Anyway, I told people I had AIDS when I met
them. Lots of people wanted to take me on as a project to
enrich their lives."

"That's not a bad thing."

"No, it's not. It's helping each other. One person
remembered me from when I was a kid. He thought he heard
that I'd gone off to live in a cave in Australia."

"There are no caves in Australia," Yale said.

"That's what I told him. He wanted me to shoot Crystal
methadrine."

"You didn't do it, did you?"

"The last time I did drugs," Peter said very slowly, "I
was in a car and there was an accident and a man on a motor-
cycle was run over. The person I was with told me to close
my eyes but I couldn't and I looked over and the man didn't
have a face. I can still see it."

"You should never do drugs anymore."

"I can't do them," Peter said, "because whenever I do
and I'm not alone in a room, I know that there are tiny holes
in the walls and there is a superior being watching me,
standing in judgment. I also think that I have tremendous
powers, and if I believe it hard enough I can make somebody
knock on the door. I get schizophrenic. Seriously. I only got
high once in Portland. I went to that bathhouse above Flossie's,
rented a VIP room, locked the door and listened to the complete tapes of *Remembrance of Things Past* with a portable
cassette player, and watched pornography, because there was
nothing else to see. Talk about incongruity."

"That's pretty funny." Yale opened his eyes and looked
at Peter seriously. "So tell me, how do you feel now?"

Peter took his shirt off to show Yale the enormous size

of the burn that the DNCB was leaving on his arm. It was puffy and yellow. "What should I do now about this?" he asked. "You said I only had to do it four times and now I have only one more treatment left."

"I think you should stop doing the DNCB immediately," Yale answered. "You've let it get too burned. I think now you should try a different T-cell booster. Why don't you try Antabuse? It's got Imuthiol in it, like DTC. I told you about it. It's very hard to get but it comes in the Antabuse that alcoholics take to make them sick when they drink. I have some written information about it that you can take to your doctor." Yale leaned back again and closed his eyes.

"Are you tired?" Peter asked again. He knew that Yale was. He pulled the blanket up over Yale's chest and sat with him for a while longer.

14

Before going to the doctor that morning Peter had bleached his hair yellow. It makes me look younger, he decided, thinking about the crease that had begun forming between his brows. And now as he sat in the designated waiting area for the Primary Care Clinic at the very hospital in which he'd been born, he felt silly about having done it.

While he waited he thought about the phone call he'd had from Yale complaining of a sudden swelling of his lymph glands, of his weight that had dropped to 128, of the grayish white lines of haziness in his eyesight. A doctor had been to see him and said he was coming down with pneumocystis pneumonia. Peter made a mental note to discuss this with his own doctor.

Peter's doctor was a young man who was an assistant to the doctor who treated most of the city's AIDS patients. When Peter came for his weekly appointment, he brought with him some of the newspaper clippings his mother had set aside. The articles came from the *New York Native,* the *Village Voice* and the *Advocate* in Los Angeles, and were about experimental treatments for AIDS. When the doctor greeted Peter on the telephone he always used his first name, Bob. This gave Peter the impression that they were contemporaries, colleagues even; they were working together. He knew his doctor felt this way, and together they would examine the newspaper articles Peter brought. He was now waiting to find out if his liver would allow him to take Antabuse.

Whenever he waited for an appointment or to fall asleep at night, Peter often conducted formal interviews with himself, in his head – about philosophy, about his past, about his relations with other people. He felt tired and cold now as his imaginary interviewer questioned him about one of the first people he knew whom he'd lost to the mysterious disease. There was this Jewish man, for example, he recalled of whom I was very fond. He was studying Greek at Columbia University and was majoring in philosophy. We worked out at the gym together. Then one day he decided to go to Italy, but the glands in his neck started to swell. He didn't go, and then he disappeared. His phone was disconnected. His name was Bruce, and as long as I stayed in New York I kept looking for him. I never found him and I feared that he'd died, but I was still hoping he'd be alive. And if he was, I believed that we'd be lovers someday again. At least, that's what I thought until the other day, when I got a letter in the mail after I'd placed an ad in the personal column of a gay newspaper. A man had written me: "I am Bruce's lover's best friend, and an acquaintance of Bruce's. As I do not know your relationship with Bruce, I have not mentioned your notice to his lover. Bruce died of KS last May, following a long, courageous struggle. As you may know, he was diagnosed with KS in the summer of 1983. Until the last 6-7 months, he led a productive and full life, and although he did not always feel well, he perservered with his work. He had the best medical care imaginable, and participated in the first Gamma Interferon tests as well as the pilot AZT tests at NIH. (Unfortunately, he could not tolerate AZT.) He was lucid until the end, engaging in complicated philosophical arguments. He completed the outline of his PhD dissertation. He was cremated and his ashes were spread according to instructions in his will. His library was also distributed as he directed." There is a poem he once wrote

to me, Peter thought, and I wish I could have it now, but it's
too late. This death had become one of the final straws for
Peter.

Peter could see his doctor suddenly approaching from
the Emergency Room and he brought the interview in his head
to a quick end.

"So how is Lake Oswego?" the doctor asked as Peter was
led into one of the tiny examining rooms.

"All right," Peter answered. He sat on the folding bed
and took off his jacket, which made him cold. He brought out
his folder of newspaper clippings.

"So what do you have for me today?" his doctor said,
smiling.

In the past week Peter's mother had cut out an article
from the *Village Voice* examining the properties of Antabuse.
He showed it to the doctor.

"I don't know anything about this," the doctor said, looking at him.

Peter took the paper back and read out loud: "Antabuse
is prescribed for alcoholics who are motivated to stay dry:
The drug, otherwise nontoxic, in the presence of alcohol causes
severe, limited illness. When Antabuse is broken down
chemically in the body, its composition is much the same as
Imuthiol, a French immune-boosting drug that is being
written about in the AIDS underground treatment network
and called DTC." He put the paper down. "I want you to
prescribe this for me," he said. "The prescribed dosage is
usually 750 milligrams once a week."

"We have to run liver tests first," the doctor said.

"Then let's run them," Peter told him, taking down his
pants to show his doctor the results of the DNCB treatments
applied to his lesions. He showed him the pink burns that
covered them. "I can't tell yet," Peter said, "if it got rid of
the lesions or not. I won't know until the scabs heal."

"I've never had a patient who has used DNCB," the

doctor admitted. "I can't tell anything yet either. But we'll make note if it works, so I can advise other patients about it. We need to have documented evidence before we can push anything."

"It worked for a friend of mine," Peter said.

The doctor scribbled something in Peter's folder.

"I also want a new T-cell count," Peter said, "I'm curious to know what condition my immune system is in."

The doctor nodded.

"You know," he said, "most patients don't know as much as you do about drug protocols."

"Most AIDS patients?" Peter questioned.

"No," the doctor admitted, "I guess people with AIDS usually know."

"They have to," Peter said politely.

"I think you should stop doing the DNCB immediately," the doctor said as Peter pulled up his pants.

"I'd already decided that," Peter answered. "I know the sores could get easily infected."

The doctor made another notation in his folder.

"What is your experience with pneumocystis pneumonia?" Peter asked once the doctor had put down his folder and filled out the prescriptions for Peter's blood test. "I have a friend who just came down with it. What are his chances?"

"About 25 percent who get it live," the doctor said matter-of-factly, and Peter was surprised that he even knew this much. "I guess," he went on, "it would depend on his immune system."

Peter felt calm, although he knew that Yale's immune system was worse than his; it was under 200.

"Now," the doctor said, "I have something for you from today's newspaper." He began reading: "The first human tests of a controversial new drug to treat acquired immune deficiency syndrome are scheduled to begin on six patients this

month at the University of Southern California. Officials at
the institute said they believe Peptide T, which is derived from
a piece of the envelope protein that surrounds the AIDS virus,
might block the whole virus from binding to the so-called T-4
helper cells, the critical immune system cells typically attack-
ed and destroyed by the virus.''

"That's fantastic," Peter said. "That was in today's paper?"

"Not only that but this." The doctor picked up the paper
again. He seemed proud to be able to report something positive
on behalf of the medical industry: "Researchers studying
patients with AIDS in New York City found that about
15 percent of them survived at least five years after diagnosis
with the disease, indicating a less dire outlook for some
patients than is commonly assumed." The doctor stopped and
put the paper down again. "I guess," he said, "if I'm going
to prescribe Antabuse for you so you can get the Imuthiol I
need to know if you're a drinker."

In regards to drinking, Kaposi's Sarcoma in some ways
had been the only thing keeping Peter in check, but he knew
there might soon enough come a time when the KS wouldn't
even matter, wouldn't even stop him from doing the things
he'd once done: If he had visible lesions, so what? He would
sit in the dark corners of bars again. He feared this would
happen to him; he feared the day that the idea of whole-
someness would seem ridiculous to him. And he knew himself
well enough to realize that all that needed to happen was one
really bad thing, like Yale getting more and more sick, and
Peter would be out the door, drinking in some bar in Portland.
I must not let my spirit get dark, he told himself.

"I'll take the Antabuse," Peter said to his doctor. This was
a serious decision because, if he drank alcohol at all, with the
medication in him, the liquor would turn to formaldehyde,
and he could die. Alcohol wasn't going to heal anything
anyway. I just have to get healthy again, he thought, but I must
not try to decide the reason why. The reason would fall apart

if he analyzed it too hard. "Get healthy for me," his mother would say, and Peter would have to admit that this could be enough of a reason. I must really be depressed now, he concluded.

"But, as it stands," his doctor told him, "I can only prescribe the Antabuse if I know you're an alcoholic. FDA rules."

Peter started to think about his father who had, after Peter's recent illness, taken to bed himself. "He's trying to get sympathy," Peter's mother told him. "He's testing me. He wants us to feel sorry for him, to see if I'll sit by his bed as I did with you." Peter's father was having a more and more difficult time; he was getting less attention from his wife and Peter's needs clearly came before his. When Peter first discussed taking Antabuse with his parents, and asked if he could use his father's prescription for it, his mother said it was necessary that his father have a physical examination in order to renew his supply. "Then, if he does," she said, "we'll also find out if he's really sick, and if there's a reason that he looks so gray." "But," Peter told her, "if he doesn't want to see a doctor I respect that. I'll get the Antabuse another way." "He'll have to see a doctor," she said, "because he'll be doing it for you. He needs the opportunity to do something for you." Peter had left it at that.

"The problem here," his doctor said finally, "is that since the FDA hasn't approved Antabuse as a treatment for people with AIDS, I probably can't give it to you unless you have a documented drinking problem."

"Well, even if I didn't, I could always say I did."

The doctor looked dubious.

"I'll get it from my father," Peter made a snap decision. "He has a drinking problem and I think there's still some Antabuse in the kitchen cupboard. But what I'd like to know is, how can we get documentation for these drugs, if the FDA is unwilling to let people try them?"

"They conduct their own tests," the doctor said.

"But not quickly enough," Peter added. He knew that gays were viewed as promiscuous and uncapable of deep lasting relationships. Why would gays be important?

"I'd be willing to take the drug Peptide T that's been in the newspapers, if I could, as a guinea pig, for experimentation, that is."

"We're not running the tests here, of course," the doctor answered. "But I'll remember that you're interested in helping with tests."

Of course I am, Peter thought. And the FDA should help me, too. Life has become a nightmare. It doesn't even resemble what it used to be. My right to be alive is being challenged — by a disease, by a government that isn't paying enough attention to it. And I have to fight this oppressor with a superhuman strength. But my worst enemy is myself. I must not let myself get negative about things the way Yale has. I must not be ashamed of my drug or alcohol behavior. I must not think that I have been a bad person. I must not think that I have only been a catalyst for other people, that I haven't done anything good myself. If I could only remain conscious, moment by moment, of how I treat other people, and myself. I must not see myself as a bad apple pretending to be good, and that it is only fitting that a person like me should have AIDS.

"I'll see you in a week." His doctor put Peter's folder under his arm.

"I mentioned that I have a friend I talked to the other day," Peter said before his doctor could leave. "He is getting really sick with pneumocystis pneumonia."

"Is he taking AZT?"

Peter scoffed. "The FDA is full of shit. You might as well admit it."

The doctor shook his head. "That I cannot do."

Peter didn't even have the courage now to ask about getting onto AL-721. I'll call him in a few days, he thought.

15

I guess it happened over the weekend," said Yale's brother, who had flown in from Miami, as Peter and he stood outside the door of Yale's hospital room. "They were giving him pain medication and then his mind started to wander. His central nervous system got infected. He was confused and incoherent. I don't even think he's conscious anymore."

I hope he isn't, Peter thought. He'd been there all morning watching Yale get worse. When he arrived at the hospital Peter was not prepared for what he saw. He caught his breath. Was *that* Yale? It was. It was Yale *ruined*. Peter could feel death in the room.

Although his eyes were open, Yale's pupils had moved up into his head so that they couldn't be seen. Peter was aware of his own eyes stinging with emotion. Seeing Yale now was like looking down and seeing his own fingers missing. He breathed in sharply.

When he picked up Yale's hand he could feel pressure on his own, but he knew it was only automatic reflexes. How could this have happened so quickly?

Yale's brother looked at the swollen body, at the big eyes. "The doctor says he has a respiratory infection, but I still don't understand why he breathes so heavily."

Yale's eyes closed.

"I don't know," Peter said. He put Yale's cold sweaty hand back. "I think maybe it's because he's congested."

"He's dying."

But Peter wasn't listening. His entire attention was focused on Yale's breathing. Panicking, he began to talk to him: "I'm going to tell you a story," he said, "about one day in New York. It was a hot Sunday at the end of spring. I dressed up a little. It was 1984, the last year when all gay people could have fun, not checked by city bathhouse or nightclub closures. I was on Christopher Street, our street. It was like a parade. The streets were filled with gay men, mostly in couples, or in groups of three or four. I was sitting in a doorway near Hudson Street. I was wearing a T-shirt from the Strand Bookstore where I worked, and I was also wearing a funny black leather German schoolboy cap. It looked like a beret but it had a brass medallion on it and I could tell people were looking at me funny. That's when I decided the world was changing for people who lived the gay lifestyle. Somebody offered me a beer and I drank it, and then I sat there all day until the sun burned my nose."

Looking at Peter as if he were an idiot, Yale's brother pushed his hands down into his pockets and left the room. When he was gone, Peter took a chair and pulled it up to the bed. He began talking more animatedly.

"I remember that day I eventually walked down to the pier. The warehouses across the street had been torn down by the city. They were famous all over the world. Anything you could imagine went on in them. You remember that."

Peter stopped long enough to take an Acyclovir pill for the white growths on his tongue. Then he continued:

"As I sat outside Sneakers Bar, with all those crusty old men with chains or whatever hanging from their belts, the lines in their faces, their potbellies — I realized an age had ended and another was beginning. I knew it then, Yale. I knew that we were on borrowed time, that a person couldn't carry on like a fool any longer. If you were drunk or indecent, people turned the other way. Either you dove head first into

your own fatal debauch, or you cleaned yourself up. It was
sink or swim. AIDS was nature's catalyst for us, saying: 'Get
it together now or die.' The warehouses at the piers closed
down. The Mineshaft and the Anvil closed in November. In
1985 all the options were thinning. People began to stay
home. People began to die.''

He looked at Yale but saw no acknowledgment. There
was only the noise of his breathing.

"It was when I realized I needed to recover something
lost that I thought about my home, about my mother. It had
been as though she didn't exist anymore. My childhood wasn't
real. It seemed as if my life had been lived by someone else
and the memory alone passed to me. I was starving myself
in that world. We had gone too far in our drug and sexual
freedom. We were living in a compulsive whirlwind. I left
my life somewhere dying in a dark back room. Nobody was
happy and we were all helpless, caught up in something that
was snowballing, something that no one understood, a movement even, that we all resisted. But when the baths closed –
we thought at first only temporarily – it was no longer
glamorous to be seen riding out the end of a party high. You
couldn't help but feel like a businessman caught in his office
with his pants down. 'Change or be ridiculed.' No, it wasn't
the general population of New York who exercised the greatest
behavior modification. It was the younger gays, the profes-
sionals, the yuppies, the born-againers, the people who'd given
up their bad habits, or had never had them to begin with.''

Peter stroked the greasy hair back from Yale's forehead.

"One of my biggest nagging impressions,'' he went on
as though Yale were listening to him, "is of working as a
secretary or a typist for a temporary agency. What drudgery
that was — and how depressing! I always wanted to get out
of high school because I hated it so much. It seemed like death
to me. But in the working world it was as bad as high
school — the alienation, the sense of playacting in a world

I held nothing but hostility for. And my biggest nagging impression was what an irony it seemed for me to lead the sort of life I did at night and then drag myself in to the so-called respectable world to try to ingratiate myself with the older people who'd been with the company all their adult lives. In reality the things I saw at night would make most of them sick to their stomachs. But I would pretend to be an aspiring secretary, with goals they would call 'sensible.' And I hated them all, every one of them; I loathed them, looked down on them, marveled at how such boring, ritualized nine-to-five lives could be satisfactory. None of them would ever get AIDS, of course, but was that any justification for the deadened existences they led? Would it have been different for me if I'd had a family, if I was heterosexual and not homosexual, if my ultimate goal as a gay man was nothing more than to make another person my mate? And what *was* my goal? Did I ever think one was necessary? 'You can do anything you want,' I used to tell people in bars, 'just so you don't feel quilty about it afterwards. Then it's stupid. That's when you've made a mistake.' I tried not to feel guilt and I rarely did. AIDS came in like a great wave and washed away the dirt. It left life clear, it's problems obvious. After AIDS I didn't care what anyone said. But it was still hard to escape the guilt. That alone is surely enough in itself to kill a person.

"How many jobs was I fired from, back then, because I couldn't make it to work after a particularly rough night? But at least I'd had fun. In temporary work you changed jobs often enough, and the shorter you stayed at one, the fewer opportunities you had to see that you were screwing up. If they kept sending you on different assignments you could always start over with a clean, new image that hadn't yet had a chance to erode. But I worked at every agency in town, and most of them grew to hate me. In their eyes, I wasn't depend-able, and being dependable was the name of the game. Of course, it didn't count that most of the people I worked for were schmucks, or treated me like one.

"One time I gave it all up, Yale, and took a job in the laundry of the St. Mark's Baths. No more neckties and slacks. I tried to remind myself that the best part about the job was that I could clean my clothes for free. The worst part was that the job paid so badly I'd begun to feel subhuman — working nights, sleeping days. I remember I read *Jane Eyre* then, and *Pride and Prejudice,* Bruce's favorite book, and then *Wuthering Heights.* When I remember that job that's what I think of most.

"So, in the morning when I got out I went to all the places the people who worked as bartenders went to relax at, before going home — the after 'after-hours' places. I remember there was one guy from a bar at the top of Christopher who intriqued me. He had tattooed designs on his face. A dark Irishman, probably from Boston, I thought at the time. I decided: He put those tattoos on just so he'd never be able to get a job in an office, no matter how hard up he was — he'd done it purposely to prevent any possibility of its ever happening, of ever having a normal life. You couldn't help but admire that courage.

"You know, the whole time I lived in New York I never owned a wallet or a watch. Never. I didn't need them. Whatever money I had would be gone the same day I got it. That was the rule. And time? Days were all that mattered. Sundays the stores closed early. I didn't even have a clock in my room.

"My roommate in the East Village called me up the other day and said he met a guy in a movie house on Fourteenth Street, and the guy took him up to Seventeenth Street and Irving, to the old rooming house where I lived. He took him to my old room where my old roommate had spent the night with me, where so much of my history in New York had occurred. 'I was in your old room,' he shouted to me over the long-distance telephone. 'I just knew you were watching me, that you were still there in that room somehow and you were laughing at me.'

"My happiest times in New York, before AIDS came along and ruined everything for all of my friends, were Sunday mornings. Those were the best, Yale, when I was alone, my blood cooled, exorcised of the passions that sent me out, from Thursday night until I dropped at midnight on Saturday, took a cab home if I was lucky, avoided my fired-up Italian landlady who always seemed to be wanting money from me. Then I'd fall on my bed with my clothes on, and it wasn't until Sunday morning that I'd start to feel human again. That was just it – we wanted our independence as gay people, the independence to lead our life-style, and yet still feel as though we belonged to the world. And more and more we didn't feel that way. AIDS only increased the alienation."

Yale's eyes were still closed. When they opened Peter knew Yale was looking at him. He could not speak. He was trying to — and then he started to get sick.

Yale's brother came back in the room and went over to the bed. "Let's call the nurse."

"No," Peter said. "Don't call a nurse."

"But why?"

"Because he's going to die, and nobody can stop that."

Yale's brother said nothing but stared at the waxy yellowing face. Then Yale seemed to stop breathing.

"He's dying right now," his brother said, panicking.

Peter tried to find Yale's pulse but could not.

"He's dead, isn't he?" the brother asked.

At that moment they both heard the terrible sound of air going up into Yale's nostrils.

"He's not dead," Peter said, but still he could find no pulse. "But he's stopped struggling."

By the time the nurses entered, Yale was gone. But Peter wasn't convinced. He seemed to detect some movement in

Yale's body. His mouth was open; his eyes were rolled up in his head.

"Is he completely dead?" Yale's distraught brother asked of the nurses.

"Yes, he's dead."

"I don't understand why his neck moved a moment ago"

"You don't always die in one moment," the nurse answered. "There's not always such a distinct line between life and death. Sometimes it takes people several hours to leave their bodies completely."

The two men were led out of the room.

"I guess he's really been dying for a long time now," the brother said.

He died like a dog, Peter thought. There was no consolation in any of this.

The two of them walked toward the window at the end of the hall. The sky was a dark blue, with a bright spot of yellow where the clouds had broken.

"I guess I had better call my relatives," Yale's brother said. "We'll have the funeral in Miami."

Peter walked aimlessly down the corridor alone. At this moment, he thought, Yale no longer exists. His body exists, but he doesn't. When he got to the exit door he opened it. For a moment he regarded the stairs. Then quickly he walked down to the street.

16

This is going to be my last meeting," the social worker informed the group. "It's hard for me," he went on to exclaim, "because this is a very real place. People don't bullshit here. This group has been through its ups and downs, but the place has always remained safe, I think, for all of us. Some of you are aware that I've been HIV positive for some time now. Recently I came down with my first opportunistic infection. For my own health's sake I'm moving to Hawaii, where my parents live. I explained this last week, so I hope this won't come as a big surprise for those of you who weren't here. Now, I think we're all aware that a member of our group died the other day."

Peter felt no relationship to the people in the room. He didn't care what anyone thought about anything. Stonily he stared out the window at the sky.

"I guess part of the difference with you leaving," one of them said to the social worker, "is that we can't take it completely personally."

Peter's expression went sour. He let his disgust show clearly in his eyes. He did not feel at all like crying. When he looked out of his eyes he felt no love for anything he could see.

"Now, why don't we each talk about our week?" The social worker turned to the man sitting next to him.

"I met someone who lives on a farm in the country close

to here," the speaker began, "and I really liked him, and when it came time to go to bed I told him that I'd been sick with pneumocystis pneumonia. And then he said he was glad I told him and that he was HIV positive, as well."

"That's really good news," the social worker said. "I think it's been very difficult for you to admit to other people that you're sick. I think that was a good lesson for you, that not everybody will reject you if you tell them you have AIDS."

"The only problem is," the man continued, "he lives in a trailer and there's only an outhouse and you have to heat the water. I was raised that way, and I don't ever want to be like that again. I dread spending the weekend with him, with absolutely no household conveniences."

Peter closed his eyes, and tried to make the voice go away. He made up a song in his head, and he heard nothing more. Eventually, he could let his eyes remain open and he wasn't distracted: he saw and heard nothing.

The first funeral Peter rembered knowing about was his great-grandmother's. She was in her late eighties when her heart gave out. The only thing he remembered about her was that when she came once to the house for tea she wore a blue and white print dress, and that she was very old. And once when he visited her, she was sitting in a chair before the window, calling "Where's my Petey-boy?" Then she was dead, and Peter was put in a day-care-center. He remembered driving away from the day-care center in his grandmother's car after the funeral. It was 1966. She was telling him about her younger brother who had spinal meningitis back in 1921. His mind had never advanced past the age of a young child. When his family went away they would have to lock him in a closet. "Why did they have to do that?" Peter had asked. "That's what people did back then," she answered. "They locked the mentally retarded up." He looked out the car window at the quiet neighborhood and wondered how many children were locked up inside the houses.

The first funeral Peter attended was his grandmother's. The last one he went to was his uncle's. He'd been driving to Las Vegas for a vacation when he had a stroke in his car; it went off the road and burst into flames. The only way his cousin could identify Peter's uncle was by the blurred tattoos on his arms.

Peter was oblivious as the next man started talking. "I've been taking out insurance policies for the past two weeks right and left. I'm going to be worth a lot. I've been getting a rash on my chest, and I've got to go to my doctor and get medication for it."

"I brought you some." Another man reached in front of Peter to pass a bottle of ointment. Peter didn't blink.

A cake was set on the table. "Farewell," it said in the frosting. Someone made a speech to their departing social worker.

Peter looked at the pieces of cake, already sliced and on plates. He thought briefly of how easy it would be to pick up a piece and, with no expression whatsoever, toss it at the window. Or he could just as easily throw it at any of the people around him. He didn't care. But that was no different from his normal impulses. Hadn't he sat quietly in a movie theater when it suddenly occured to him how easy it would be to reach out and grab the hair of the person before him? To sit at a bar and for no apparent reason pour a drink into his own lap? Or to slit his wrist thoughtlessly with a sharp razor? After his grandmother's funeral, with his pinstripe suit on, he actually jumped into the lake.

I should eat a piece of cake, he thought, remembering how he believed he was too skinny as a child, always promising himself after a big meal to continue to keep his stomach as full as possible. He'd felt so insecure about his thinness that he wore his jacket indoors all through grade school. It took severe promptings from his teachers to get him to take it off. In junior high he wore a wind breaker, which was slightly less obvious. Even now summer was his least favorite season. Did it have anything to do with the fact that he had to wear less clothing then? Eat the cake. Yes, eat it. But he did not. The members of the group reached for their slices and began to eat.

"I'm still feeling shaky, or at least my hands are," someone else said. "I haven't gone to my Narcotics Anonymous or the Alcoholics Anonymous meetings. A friend of mine slept with someone who has AIDS, and then gave it to his lover, because he didn't know the man he met was sick. He feels horrible that he could have given it to his lover."

"I flew to Washington, DC, to the NIH," said another voice, "and I've been in the hospital for two weeks. My friends were calling up my mother, asking her: 'Is this it? Is this it?' We both laughed. I had a roommate, though, who was the perfect Southern gentleman. He was showing me some before-and-after pictures of himself. His face was almost black in the early pictures, and his nose was completely disfigured. I was so upset I cried. But the interferon worked. When he was discharged he had no lesions on his face at all. Nothing was visible. I was so heartened. The doctors found a few bumps behind my ears and they're testing them. I just laughed when they told me. 'So, what is it going to be now?' I asked. 'Some mysterious cancer or what?' My thighs and hips were so swollen from the morphine shots that they couldn't even get the morphine to my blood stream."

Peter felt as if a hammer were hitting him on the head, pushing him down. He didn't try to smile, even when the other people in the group laughed, made a joke, or giggled. It was as if he were on drugs.

"Keep your church out of my crotch."

Peter was startled. Someone was talking about a sign they'd seen at the rally in Washington, DC, in October. Peter thought about this for a long time, until he heard another person saying:

"I have collected furniture all my life, and now I just feel like another piece of furniture in my own house."

This is absurd, Peter thought. People say the stupidest things when they're expected to be profound! He tried not to think; all his equilibrium was at stake when he did. He tried not to think about Yale.

He listened as two people mentioned that they'd formerly been drinkers and takers of drugs, that during this period they had had very little self-appreciation.

"Ever since Randy Shilts's book on AIDS came out a month ago, telling the world that the government and the newspapers really screwed up, that they let the AIDS epidemic get so far out of hand, there's been stuff in the papers every-day. Did anybody see today's paper?"

"I saw the paper the other day," someone replied, "about those drugs that disrupt the formation of sugar molecules in AIDS-infected cells. People have been using the drugs to control blood-sugar levels.

"What I read," the man went on, "said that the NIH was using something called Peptide-11 to treat KS and that it stops cancer cells from penetrating the walls of blood vessels and invading organs. It stops the cancer cells from sticking to the vessel walls, and won't let the cancer eat through them. People aren't going to die anymore."

Peter tried to contain his anger. It's funny how sleep works, he thought. Several hours of unconsciousness, or of having your eyes closed, makes you able to go on and not fall apart. It makes you able to wake up in the morning and say, I can go on. What got me down yesterday may not to-day, you can say. When you sleep you are repairing yourself emotionally and physically, body and soul. Who knows? If a person could take naps whenever he wanted, all through the day, maybe he'd find very little to get worked up about. He could be so much more level-headed. In the morning you can always think clearly. You have more courage than at night.

With that morning clarity he could know the truth about every situation and could see how people view themselves in relation to AIDS. But he couldn't put these things into words. He knew that if he could sleep he would feel better, but he had not been able to sleep much since he went to the hospital and saw Yale die. Today nothing mattered. He could tell no one about this because the only person...*Stop.*

Peter thought of the argument he'd had over the telephone that morning with his doctor. "I can't prescribe AL-721 for you," he'd said. "I can't give it to anyone through the hospital. It hasn't been FDA-approved; I don't care how much success you guys have been having with it. My hands are tied. You'll have to get it on the black market. It's common knowledge that AL-721 in Israel is the real stuff. What you find in America doesn't meet any standards. You can try, of course, but your health insurance won't pay for it."

"A friend came looking for me after I was fired," one of the voices in Peter's AIDS group droned on, "and my boss told him that I was no longer with them. My friend began crying, because he mistakenly assumed that I had died. It was funny, in a sad way."

But Peter was thinking... "Old age has more disadvantages than advantages," an aging relative had once informed him. "As long as I know people who are older than I am and I see their failings, then I only have to see myself as 'approaching' old age." If there was any way at all to do it gracefully, Peter wanted to live to be a very old man. But he wanted to have control over his senses, too, particularly over his mind. Dementia was a fairly common result of the AIDS virus, and he feared this end more than most of the others. Getting along compatibly with people was hard enough ordinarily, without something extra to make it worse. Senility in old people was rarely acceptable socially; senility in a young person was even worse. "At least," the relatives had said that one sunny morning after a church service long ago, "when you're old or dying, you really do learn how to live for the moment, and not to worry about any more than you have to. You care so much less about what other people think." Yes, these were the good things about living to be old, Peter thought. And what of the old people who repeated themselves, who made you sleepy to listen to? Is that something he wanted for himself? Did he really care?

All any of us in this room really wants, he thought, is just a little more time. That's all. And most of society may not give a damn about that. But we can't give up and let society just put us away. We need a little more patience, I know. My mom says, "Just hold on until there's a cure, that's all you have to do. Don't give up yet."

I must fight back my anger. I must not blame the people in this room. How can I? These people don't show real compassion for each other. All they present are their fears. Maybe Yale showed compassion, but these people. . . .

Go steady, he reminded himself, or you'll do or say something that will hurt people. You don't have to laugh if you don't find something funny. You don't have to smile if you don't want to. Do as your Aunt said: "Live just for now. Live among people as if you were never to see them again, as if every moment meant something. Don't lose heart now."

He looked around the room. These people mean you no harm. They may not be upset enough about Yale, but that's only because they didn't know him. They are too afraid for themselves to think about anyone else right now. People's failings are usually a result of lack of experience. Society does not suffer because someone is an outcast. How can society know what you feel as an individual, or know the feeling of dying of a disease that is killing you, while a higher power looks on and does nothing?

This, he decided, no matter what I do, will be my last AIDS meeting. They can go ahead and assign a new social worker, but this is *it* for me.

What should I do next? he wondered. He remembered that Yale had wanted him to go to a Vedanta meeting, but Peter knew next to nothing about Hindu religion or meditation. He didn't laugh at it or dismiss it, he'd just never looked into it. What would it take for him to get interested, to do something? It took a famous person to die before the general population woke up to AIDS in 1985. And it took heterosexuals contracting the disease before the major newspapers would even report that the virus existed. The problem was that not enough famous people had died for people to become hysterical. It was simply thousands of people like Yale.

The social worker was ending the discussion. "I think what's important for us to do today is to discuss our individual feelings about what Yale's death meant to us. How does it bring out our own fears? How does it alter our hopes?"

The discussion went around the room. None of what was said made any sense to Peter. When it came his turn, he thought for a long time. He was the last person to speak. No one in the group knew that he and Yale had been friends. But Peter said it anyway: "I don't think he knew. I loved him."

"And we'll all miss you, too." someone told the social worker. "We wish you luck."

Peter bolted for the door.

17

The altar itself was a photograph of one of the gurus, looking rather scraggly, Peter thought, against a background of velvet. There were candles with pink and red flower bouquets on either side. The only time he'd ever seriously prayed to God was when his stomach pains and his digestive tract problems became acute. Then he had pleaded and begged for them to stop.

In his hand, he carried a scrap of paper on which Yale had written the address of the Vedanta Society. He examined it while he waited for the first speaker to begin. The he took out the article his mother had cut from the morning paper. He skimmed it because he'd agreed to read it:

"Zaire televsion, playing a videotape of a news conference where a new treatment for AIDS was announced Sunday said that the 'suspense is lifted.' But little information was given about the drug developed by doctors in Zaire and Egypt. Doctors said their new treatment, called MM1, had improved the condition of some AIDS victims in a 6 month test . . . The doctors told reporters and diplomats at the news conference that an AIDS remedy must be capable of destroying the virus and restoring the body's immune system without being toxic . . . Many African nations are sensitive to theories that the deadly disease originated on the continent."

Stories, stories, stories. He was becoming tired of them.

He looked about at the congregation in the meeting hall:

a few single men, mostly single women, and some couples. A man had begun to read an article about divine love in humans, saying the "swami" had requested him to do so to "warm everyone up."

When the swami came out, Peter was surprised. He was a funny old man from another era — a Hindu Moses with a sense of humor. He was also familiar with the fine art of dramatics. He spoke, occasionally violent, about the mundane, illusory, transitory world. He looked like a brown-faced Edward G. Robinson, with dark circles under his eyes. He was crouched over, with an orange shawl draped theatrically over his shabby gray suit. He spoke initially in Sanskit, or so Peter guessed. When the people laughed at what the swami said, Peter could not even understand why. They must come there a lot, he decided, to understand his accent. As he listened he started to get a toothache.

With his hands across his belly, the swami lifted an index finger to make a point and mumbled his dialogue. He spoke of Plato, the Bonneville Dam on the Columbus River ("Your scientists have done well there"). His topic, loosely, was the Path to Enlightenment.

Peter looked at the eerie glow from the red and blue windows that cast color onto his hands. A piano played a slow, troublesome melody. He thought it sounded like the theme to *Love Story* on TV.

"In order to see God" — Peter could barely decipher the swami's words — "you must renounce. You must go to an illumined teacher who teaches self-control. Be the master of your senses. You are all unconsciously enlightened souls. You must be made conscious. Whether you know it or not, you are divine. Essence is infinite knowledge and bliss."

When the swami began speaking of physical pain, Peter stood up and crept out of the hall. At the door he bought a copy of the Bhagavad Gita and left.

As he silently rode in his father's car (his father was wear-

ing a bath robe and driving with bare feet), Peter looked at
the houses along the Willamette River. That's a lonely house,
he thought. And that's a house for a divorced woman. A
hermit lives here. A small happy nuclear family lives there.
Honest people. That's an apartment for a young married
couple who drink beer on Saturday nights. . . . He was not
thinking about the talk he'd just attended; in his mind he'd
decided it had been a failure.

As they entered the small town in which Peter's family
lived, he noted that it was growing very quickly. Time was
passing. He knew that in the twenties Lake Oswego had been
a resort where people came to stay during vacations. When
Peter was born, there were only a small number of families,
roughly ten thousand. But today the population was double
or triple that.

As Peter stared out the window at the street, the lanes
seemed to overlap. One side of the road curved, and it
appeared as if there were two lanes where in fact there was
only one. He concentrated hard. My eyesight, he thought, I
hope isn't getting worse all of a sudden. To avoid hysterics
he had to think about something else. He closed his eyes and
imagined that in his hand he held the tubes of blood his
doctor routinely sent with him to the lab. He had to carry
them back to the nurse's office, always amazed at how warm
the blood felt. This came out of me, he'd think.

Finally, when Peter was alone he began flipping through the
pages of the Bhagavad Gita. Nothing seemed to speak to him.
Thinking quickly, he pulled once more from his drawer
Neoma's old book, *The Autocrat of the Breakfast-Table*. He
was not sure what he was searching for, but whatever it was,
he hoped it might bring him illumination.

The more we study the body and the mind, the more we find both to be governed, not by, but according to laws, such as we observe in the larger universe. You think you know all about walking, don't you, now? Well, how do you suppose your lower limbs are held to your body? They are sucked up by two cupping vessels, and held there as long as you live, and longer. At any rate, you think you move them backward and forward at such a rate as your will determines, don't you? On the contrary, they swing just as any other pendulums swing, at a fixed rate, determined by their length. You can alter this by muscular power, as you can take hold of the pendulum of a clock and make it move faster or slower; but your ordinary gait is timed by the same mechanism as the movements of the solar system.

He continued patiently:

I think you will find it true, that, before any vice can fasten on a man, body, mind, or moral nature must be dibilitated. The mosses and fungi gather on sickly trees, not thriving ones; and the odious parasites which fasten on the human frame choose that which is already enfeebled.

This isn't working, he thought. He turned to the back of the book.

Therefore, my aged friend of five-and-twenty, or thereabouts, pause at the threshold of this particular record, and ask yourself seriously whether you are fit to read such revelations as are to follow.

He laughed, and put the book down. How could Neoma

have found any solace in this book when she was dying?
How can I?

From his shelf he took down a copy of the Bible. If I'm
to believe what everyone says, he thought, there's got to be
something in here. He read from Ecclesiastes.

> What is man, what purpose does he serve? What is
> the good in him, and what the bad? Take the number
> of a man's days: a hundred years is very long. Like a
> drop of water from the sea, or a grain of sand, such
> are these few years compared with eternity.

That's no help, he thought. He read a little further.

> Do not abandon yourself to sorrow, do not torment
> yourself with brooding. Gladness of heart is life to a
> man, joy is what gives him length of days.

Dreamily, Peter remembered his first days at church. While
he attended Sunday School his parents went to the big church.
His father was always an usher, even then, Peter suspected,
because it made him feel important.

The Episcopal church was a big building, the house of
God. There were passageways under it and along the side, or
so it seemed to Peter who found the whole thing mysterious
and forbidding to begin with. One of the rooms was furn-
ished as Peter imagined the Presidential suite at the White
House to be.

After Sunday School, Peter, who wore a navy blue jacket
with a clip-on bow tie and a very short haircut, would go
into the big church and search out his parents for the
remainder of the service. His mother would be wearing a fur,
a new strange hat, white gloves. She was pretty.

Communion was allowed when Peter was older. He tried

saving up the wafer in his mouth for as long as possible. This was "discipline." He imagined that the hot sip of wine made him drunk.

Church, no matter what Peter's age, had always been an ordeal. When he was very small he imagined that his eyes were the lens of a camera, and that he represented a television station. Whatever he looked at was the picture that the camera saw, so that he could always keep his vision on interesting people and make his frames artistic. He'd roam the audience long enough to see that everyone was fidgety, men in collars straining their necks, his own mother flicking the underpart of her long nails.

His parents went only to the Episcopal church. "It was your grandmother who picked it out," his mother once explained. "Her parents were Baptists, and when your grandmother was an adult she wanted to find a church that was both more reasonable and more social. When she got into real estate she found that with all of its social aspects, the Episcopal church made it easier for her to make business contacts. It was sort of like at the country club. She was always a people person."

Peter's father had joined the church when he married Peter's mother. "I do everything her way," he often said.

When Peter's grandmother died, and they went to the funeral service and saw the coffin in the aisle, it was the last time Peter's mother insisted that the family go to church. As far as Peter could remember they never went again. But church had been a regular thing in their lives up to that point. Peter even joined the choir.

The minister's daughter was mean, he remembered. She was in Peter's Sunday School class. She said bad things to the more insecure children, and the teachers often had to discipline her. The minister's wife played a guitar, wore flowers in her hair, and made the children learn the words to "Morning Has Broken" by Cat Stevens. She made felt banners with

words of inspiration pasted on them. They lived in a cheap
shack like house on McVey. One day she and the minister got
a divorce, and he went to Hawaii. Peter remembered all of
this very clearly.

When Peter's grandmother died, the priest came to their
house that afternoon, sat with Peter in the music room, and
quizzed him about his relationship with his grandmother.
"She was someone special for you, wasn't she?" he asked.
Peter was morose, tired from crying. He put his head on his
mother's shoulder. He had a rip in his pants at the knee. As
the priest continued to ask him questions Peter stuck his finger
inside the hole and kept pulling it, making the tear bigger and
bigger.

One of the ministers at the church was fired. Peter
remembers, in the early 1970s. He had long hair and spoke
once about the Vietnam War; he said it was too bad that so
many people had to die. An old lady stood and very pointed-
ly stalked out of the church. "It's my birthday," she said to
the usher, Peter's father. "And I don't want to hear about this
stuff." It was during the days when feelings about Vietnam
ran high. "It's a conservative town," Peter's mother explained. Peter didn't know exactly what she meant, he just knew
that all old people were like that — all old people, that was,
except for his grandmother.

Peter looked through the Bible once more, and then put
it back up on the dusty shelf.

18

"Sara only talks to me when she wants something."

Peter turned sympathetically to his father, who was sitting at the card table by the fireplace, working on a jigsaw puzzle. They were alone.

"Only if she wants a ride, or if she wants me to do something for her."

"Dad," Peter said, "I hope I don't come across to you that way. What I've always wanted to say to you is that you don't seem that receptive to people's emotions. You have your insecurities, too, I know, but you never made it easy for anyone to talk to you."

When Peter's father worked on a jigsaw puzzle, it reminded Peter of someone digging a ditch, filling it up and digging another – a supreme waste of time. He tried not to be judgmental.

"When I think about the things I'd do differently . . . his father said, as he lit a cigarette and shook his head.

"Dad," Peter said, pulling the blanket up tighter around himself, "I'm going to need your help a little, and I don't want you to feel that I'd ask you to do me favors and at the same time not approve of you. The way I feel now, you and Mom are my best friends. I don't see that many people anymore. I want it that way. You two are the only people who really understand me. You know what I want and need." He was giving his father a little more credit than he ordinarily would,

but it was important. If he didn't make his father feel included, then his father never would be. There was a long overdue
need for change.

Recently Peter had read somewhere that most Kaposi's
Sarcoma patients generally lived for twenty-one months after
their first sign of a lesion. That means I have roughly four
months, he thought. In his mind it was time that he came to
a complete understanding with his family. Every day in the
papers, scientists were contradicting themselves about the
lifespan of people with AIDS. In Peter's own studies of his
friends, he'd found the twenty-one-month theory generally to
be true.

"Dad," he said, "I think it's important that you know
I like you."

"When I was in high school," his father started to say
without any apparent connection, "when the other kids went
down to the river, I worked as a mail boy. I didn't get to go
to the river and sail on the boats. I was twenty before I got
to ride in the stock-car races. I swore that someday I would
live on a lake, have a boat, an expensive car, a nice house.
At any price. Can you blame me for wanting those things?"

Peter's father was opening an old wound.

"I don't blame you for that," Peter said. "It's just that
it always seemed so hollow to me. When I was growing up
we were always pretending, always playing at being rich. We
weren't really rich, not then. And then when Mom got all that
money, it still seemed false to me. I didn't understand why
we needed to worry so much about what other people thought
of us. I used to daydream about being poor. I thought it was
more romantic to live in a shack, to feel the things that real
people felt. I wanted to live life more, I didn't want to
be always putting distance between myself and the things that
were hard."

"I knew about the things that were hard," his father said.

"Did you start drinking in high school?"

"That was it."

"Did your father drink, too?"

"I don't remember my father," he answered. "All I remember is a dark room and him in bed."

"I heard he went crazy."

"He hallucinated in the end," his father said. "He used to warn my mother to be careful, that the house didn't have a roof, that there were workmen up there and she could get hurt if something fell. He put his hand through a window, too. That was in Laurelhurst where you were born. Same house."

"I just remember red carpet," Peter said.

"It was blue."

Peter's concentration faded, and he found himself thinking about a Christmas program in the third grade. Each of his classmates had made drawings that were shown on an opaque projector. At the end of the presentation they showed Peter's drawing, which was of Snoopy levitating at the top of a Christmas tree. They left the image on the screen for a long time, and Peter had felt a certain exhiliration. He was trying to recapture the feeling, and wondering why he'd stopped drawing in grade school. He'd been good at it, and had even attended classes at the Portland Art Museum, and been taught by the nuns at Marylhurst College. He wanted to tell his father; "We all had our dreams. Because things didn't turn out as we'd planned, it doesn't mean they turned out wrong."

"But at the Port of Portland," his father was saying, "I burned out. It was those martinis that I had with all my clients. I had to give speeches and entertain clients every day. There was so much pressure."

And when did I first start drinking? Peter thought. Then he remembered Phillip, who'd come from Wisconsin. The beer capital of America. Phillip collected beer cans of every brand he could find. One of his bedroom walls was obscured by stacks of them. Another friend collected Beatles pictures and posters; one of his own walls was covered as well. Peter had bright wallpaper that he had chosen at age twelve. As he got older, the wallpaper gave him a headache. He covered it with pictures.

To this day Peter hated beer. He hated to be drunk, as well, but he understood about his father's pressure and he knew well enough now that alcohol could neutralize the pressure temporarily. But it was like a loan from a bank that you would eventually have to pay back — and with high interest rates.

"Nothing seemed to work out after that," his father said. "All the firms I worked for fell apart or went bankrupt."

"Things haven't worked out for a lot of us," Peter found himself replying. "I wanted to know what it was like to live on the edge. I wanted to get scared a little, and now look what's happened. I don't think I ever stopped and asked: What am I getting myself into? Nobody knew that there was a virus out there just waiting to become an epidemic."

"You didn't know," his father repeated.

"But the point here is. . ." Peter suddenly could not think of what the point was. He made one up instead. "The point is that nobody in this house can judge anyone else. What we've got to do now is stick together and help each other." It was the same thing Yale had said to him.

"Neither of us may live that much longer," his father admitted.

"We may and we may not," Peter said. "But we probably won't. That's why I want to try to make a conscious effort to enjoy myself, not to waste any more time."

Still, it was hard to forget certain negative memories, even if he didn't often think about them. There was the father who would walk into a room and turn off the radio if he didn't like the music one of his children was listening to. There was the father who, when guests arrived, ordered his children to refill glasses, to bring things from the kitchen, and then go to their rooms so they would not be in the way. "Now get out of here," his father would growl at Sara and Peter. There was the mother who didn't always protest her husband's treatment of their children, but who once stood between Peter and his father to protect him from blows. "I was afraid he was going to kill you," she'd said later. There was also the father who, because he did not like his children's dog, took it away one day and set it loose on the other side of the lake. There was the father who ordered his children out of the room when he came home from work so he could discuss his day with his wife uninterrupted by children. "It was all lies anyway," Peter's mother would say later. "He didn't say anything, he just drank." And there was the father who told his children to go up to the house when they were all down at the lake, sitting on the dock, and bring him more wine.

Threats. Peter remembered them most: confidences he'd shared with his Dad, who only turned around and betrayed them to everyone else. He taught his son how to drive, and then disconnected the spark plugs so that Peter couldn't use the car when he wanted to. "It just doesn't seem to want to start today," his father would lie, tapping here and there with a hammer on the engine.

Peter had much more to forget than his father. "It's not easy to raise children," he'd heard enough adults say. Peter had made up his mind a long time ago never to have any. Cruelty couldn't be avoided. Maybe nobody got along with anyone else. We only pretend to.

"Your father," Peter's mother had once said, "never had a father around while he was growing up, so he didn't know how to be one. I don't think he knew what he was doing with you. He thought it was going to be easy, so that all he needed was to tell you or Sara what he wanted of you, and that you'd obey, that you'd never question anything."

Peter looked over at his father, who was chain-smoking,

putting pieces of the puzzle together. He felt no animosity toward him. Peter was sitting with him voluntarily, something he'd never have chosen to do in the past. Things had changed. He wondered if his father was afraid of death. He didn't seem to be. Maybe it was an attitude he picked up after fighting in Korea. But part of Peter didn't believe that his father was scared. There was a difference between being afraid of death and not wanting to die. Not wanting to die was something you felt when you were in a beautiful place. Being afraid of death was what happened when you went to bed at night and couldn't conceive that in six months you wouldn't be *anywhere*.

Peter's mother had said that his father had expressed an interest in being buried in a nearby cemetery. "No one in our family has been buried in this city." he'd said, "and my grandfather came here in the 1880s. My father was a postman, my uncle was a sheriff. I'm in real estate. We developed this town." Speeches like this from his father made Peter impatient. What did prestige matter when it was false anyway. Did anybody really know or care who his grandfather was? Didn't the police shake their heads in bafflement when Peter's father waved to them. "All I know," his mother said one day, "is that if he is buried in that graveyard, I'll have to drive by it every day on the way to the store, and see his big fat tombstone."

Peter realized how easy it was to criticize his father. The truth was that Peter loved him, and did not pity him. He is me, Peter thought. My father is no more himself than he is me. We're part of the same person. To hate him is to hate myself.

He reached over and played with a piece of his father's jigsaw puzzle.

Peter's mother entered the room. "How are my boys?" she asked cheerfully.

"Fine," Peter said.

She sat next to him on the couch and turned on the television with the remote control.

"Where's Sara?" Peter asked.

"She was coming up the stairs a little while ago. I think she's in the kitchen." Peter's mother took out her balls of yarn and began to knit.

"Would you like to help me with the puzzle?"

Peter looked at the picture his father was putting together. It was of a white house with trees in front, and a car. "I'm not very good at that sort of thing," he apologized. "You already filled in the easy parts."

Sara came into the room and sat down to watch a movie on TV. Neither Peter nor his mother was very interested in it. Sara had her head back, plates of food on either side of her.

Peter found a piece of puzzle with sky and a splash of red on it. He added it to the top of the chimney.

"Two points," said his father.

It was hard to imagine that at one time Peter's father had been an athlete. When Peter was in junior high his father had been a basketball coach. In Boy Scouts he'd helped Peter with his written tests, too. And Peter advanced through the ranks quicker than the others his age. They'd resented him, of course. Today things were not that much different: whenever Peter went into Portland someone who knew him from his teenage years would say to all present: "His parents are rich. He comes from the suburbs." Peter had told none of these friends that he had AIDS; he didn't see them often enough, nor did he trust them. They'd made fun of him when he was the youngest at parties. If he told them he had AIDS there was no knowing what the reaction might be. Besides, he seldom went into Portland. Since returning to Oregon, he'd hardly seen anyone. Yale was the only person he'd come to know. And now he wasn't interested in making new friendships: people died, once you got to know them.

His sister sat across from him. She said nothing.

"Do you want to go for a walk?" his mother asked his father.

"Whatever you want," Peter's father nodded. Together they left the room.

Peter felt that it was a plan; his parents had deliberately left him alone with Sara.

He stared at the TV. It was a stupid movie but his sister seemed to be enjoying it. I can't talk to her, he thought. I know she'd answer me if I asked her a question but what's the point of talking unless she makes it known that she wants to talk, too? She didn't seem to care.

"People who have Kaposi's Sarcoma usually live twenty-one months after their diagnosis." Peter wanted to shout this at her. We're wasting time! Every minute counts when we're together! Let's make use of it!

Except for the noise from the television the room was quiet.

Maybe, he thought, this time isn't being wasted, maybe this time is being spent perfectly. There were certain things in life that never changed. One of them was Sara, who would always be sarcastic and aloof. In a way, he could accept this and appreciate her. At least he was going to try . . .

"I'm sorry about what happened to your friend Yale."

"Thank you." Peter was dumbfounded. Maybe she does have a heart, he thought, brightening. Maybe she hasn't died; maybe she's still Sara, my sister that I remember from ten years ago, the one who used to take me by the hand for a walk and say, "It's good to be out of the house, isn't it?"

She continued to watch television.

"Is it a good movie?" he asked.

"I've seen it twice."

He watched the movie and tried not to criticize it. There was a football coach who lived for the sport. He tried to instill this determination in his team. "Football," he said, "is my life." This kind of thinking is what I'm up against, Peter thought. Competition encourages the fighting instinct. He struggled for a moment, and then asked: "So how is your boyfriend? He hasn't been around at all, has he?"

"He's doing something else now," she said, not appearing to be annoyed at the interruption.

He understood this to mean that they'd broken up. "Is that good or bad?" he asked.

"It's all right."

She's lying, he thought. He tried another tactic. "Weren't you interested in marrying him?"

"Look," she said, not taking her eyes from the screen, "I'm sorry you have AIDS. Isn't that what you really want to talk about?"

"It wouldn't hurt me," he said, not missing a beat. "Do you want to talk about anything at all?" Now she'll be even more defensive, he thought.

"I don't care," she said.

He took the plunge: "I wish we had better communication," he said.

"About what?" She lit a cigarette.

"C'mon, Sara," he said, "you've got to admit it's not normal that we rarely talk anymore. You remember when Grandma was alive, we were best friends?"

"That was a long time ago."

He wondered if she really remembered. "We've both changed since then, but I think we still have things to say to each other. At least I like to think so. I don't know why not."

"Talking is easier for you than it is for me."

"Dad says the same thing."

There was a long silence.

"Can't we try, Sara?" he asked.

Sara seemed to be hating every minute. "We can try," she said finally.

"Okay," he asked, "Do you love me?"

She waited. "Yes."

"Do you think there's any hope for our family?"

."I feel," she said struggling for words, "like you're tearing me apart. Like you're trying to teach me something when I don't want to be taught. I just want to be left alone."

"I just want to be better friends," he told her, "like we used to be."

"I know you don't think so," she said, "but I think we always have been."

"Do you really think so? I'm sorry about your boyfriend," he said. "He made you happy, didn't he?"

"I didn't talk to him enough, either, I guess."

"Maybe he just didn't give you the chance to."

She looked up at him. "And maybe he did." She stood up.

"Going to bed?" he asked.

She nodded. "Some things are just harder for me than they are for you," she said. "Can't we leave it at that?"

"We can," he said.

19

O n his way to the kitchen one cold afternoon in December, Peter stopped to pull off one of the yellow flowers in a vase by the window. He looked at it carefully. Then he held it up to the light. He saw his father crossing the lawn and heading for the boathouse and instinctively crumpled up the flower. Why did I have to do that? he wondered.

When his father had gone, Peter looked out at the lake. When you get AIDS or any fatal disease there is always a lot of talk about denial, he thought. At one point he'd been so unhappy and depressed that he was certain he could never have been accused of denial. Yet what about now? If he was to have fun, would someone tap him on the shoulder and ask him if he was in a state of denial? Denial, he thought, is about as subjective as you can get. Can't a person drink, for example, all he wants, in full view of his situation, and not be called a denier? Perhaps denial referred more to the person who meant to get well but went on drinking heavily when he knew drinking would only make him worse. But what of the man who drinks, knowing full well what he is doing? He is self-destructing. But why is it that if I'm laughing or having a good time there are people who will say I'm avoiding something? Who says that a person who gets AIDS has to die, anyway? One of the important things is that a person dying of AIDS should stop referring to himself as a person dying of AIDS but rather a person living with it. It was an important semantic distinction. Even though I have AIDS he thought, it doesn't necessarily mean that I don't have to do laundry anymore, or renew my driver's license, or give up on life.

He got up from his seat by the window and went back to bed. There he began reading about one man's view on AIDS as a widespread spiritual dysfunction. The poet James Broughton said in a magazine: "The thing I can't get over is that it's related to the most intimate contact between two people, and the fact that *that* becomes a disease. It's terrifyingly symbolic of something. One really has to think about this. Exchanging vital fluids – think of what that means. Of course you do this! Of course you should if there's a deep rapport or love. We share not only our soul but our vital selves as well." Broughton went on: "AIDS is very much connected to the larger plague on all levels. They don't know where it comes from, but I think it's part of the poisoning of the whole of human life and of the planet. And here it is the homosexual society which is being sacrificed to make people aware of it."

Peter felt that what he was reading was probably very near to the truth.

"One of the things about Americans particularly," the article said, "is that with anything that's a slight imbalance, like a headache, they must run and take a pill. The slightest symptom, they must get rid of it. This is not at all the way to understand life. The important thing is not just to get rid of AIDS. What is it telling us?"

Peter put the magazine away and felt his body aching under the blanket. "Now I can't think anymore," he said aloud. It's amazing how the days just stack up on one another. I get so tired. He began to remember one day as a child, when he picked up a teddy bear and kissed it. As he'd put it into the closet with all of his other old toys, he'd said to it: "I won't love you anymore, because I'm growing up now. In a year you won't mean anything to me. So just remember: I love you, but now I have to put you away." It occurred to Peter that he had always been in the habit of denying affection.

"What I could never understand about you," his sister had once told him, "is how you like strangers more than you do your family. Strangers are strangers."

"Strangers understand me," he answered. "It's my family that doesn't understand me. Strangers aren't threatening in a way that you and Dad and sometimes Mom seem to be."

"That's because they don't love you."

That was one of Sara's smartest perceptions.

"Strangers accept you as you are," Peter tried to explain. "If you are heading down a wrong path, they won't have to pay the consequences. It's not they who will have to suffer by your actions. If what I sometimes say makes you and Dad uneasy, that is your problem and not mine. But I want to make it easy for all of us. I want us to communicate. But we never will. We will only learn how to be more polite. We'll learn to hide from one another more successfully."

It was a topic of conversation that rarely occurred, but when it did Sara and Peter's parents fell back from it, realizing the ultimate division that was occurring, the pulling apart and the pushing away. The concept of "strangers" was something one knew at home in one's own family.

He thought about his father. If he were dead, Peter's life would be easier. If Peter were dead his father's life would be easier, too; He'd have his wife all to himself, twenty-four hours a day. "Your father bothers me more than you do," his mother confessed. But what could be done at this point? "We just have to go on and make the best of it." Peter must try not to lose sight of his own self-interest. He must not let his family affect him so much.

Alone, he was thinking again about his own probable death: I would like someone who loves me to set me out on a cement table, he thought, preferably, in the woods, douse

me all over with gasoline, and then light me up. Hopefully
I would burn completely, so that even my skeleton would turn
to ashes. But since that is perhaps too much to hope for, my
friend would have to use a mallet to crunch up my bones.
From there they would need to use a sifter. When at last my
ashes are truly ashes, fine and smooth as a pile of cocaine,
I would like my mother to take them to the beach and leave
them in a pile before one of the biggest waves.

But could he ask his mother to do this? Already, her
sadness resembled the weariness of a woman who had gone
on for too long with no sleep.

Instead of tombstones, he continued thinking, everyone
who believes he's to die ought to plant a tree somewhere and
show it to a friend. Then after he's dead the tree will grow
and people can see it as a personal symbol.

He remembered that before his grandmother died, they'd
planted an apple tree. He'd watched this tree grow, and when
recently the lot was sold and he had been diagnosed, he went
back to it. He realized that this had been the plan all along:
they'd planted something together to grow. But the apple tree
was torn up when Peter went to visit it. The field had been
cleared.

"The art of medicine consists of amusing the patient while
Nature cures the disease," Voltaire wrote long ago. When
Peter's first medical treatments had begun a year before, in
New York, he'd gone to a ninety-year-old doctor who gave
him injections of sheep cells or hormones. After that he tried
Naltrexone, which was used primarily for treating heroin ad-
dicts. The Antabuse hadn't given him anything. A week ago
he'd ordered a kilo of AL-721, the drug from Israel, that looked
like hard frozen peanut butter, but it was still too early to
judge whether or not it had done him any good. Not smoking or drinking for several months hadn't hurt — that much
he knew. And beside AZT, what was left? Whether he lived
was not a question of luck. It was up to him to make each

moment a new beginning. He must not give in to the hoplessness that Yale had.

The people whom Peter had met who were trying to cure themselves of AIDS had lately been sharing the recordings of a metaphysical healer from California. Her "health tapes" were in vogue that year, and someone from Los Angeles had sent him one. He listened to the tape and found that the basic axiom was that illness served as a lesson. "I believe," the healer said, "that all illness is self-created. Not that we say, 'I want to have this illness,' but we create a mental atmosphere where this disease can grow and flourish. Our internal mental dialogue reacts in every cell in the body." As he listened to the tape, he suddenly couldn't stop smiling. He laughed at the thought that what the woman was saying could be true. "The universe will support what you choose to believe about yourself." He listened carefully: "Notice what you are thinking at this moment. Do you want this thought to be creating your future? Is it negative or positive?" He repeated out loud when the voice asked him to say: "I am willing to release the pattern in me that has created this condition. I choose to get well." In healing myself of AIDS, he thought, it is also an opportunity to make my life better.

It's sort of as if life itself was offering me an ultimatum, he thought: be enlightened or die. The process of healing himself would be a long odyssey.

He knew that he had to forgive the people toward whom he'd held deep resentments. He had to forgive his father, his sister; he had also to forgive himself. But how am I going to change the world so that people will accept me as good and not bad because I'm homosexual? It's boring to be like everybody else, he concluded, and being different isn't bad. Just because people say that I'm bad, does that really mean that I am? There must be a reason for gay people to exist. We must have something to teach.

He lay back. "I choose to live," he kept repeating to

himself. Nothing is stronger than I am. Not only must I keep my body healthy, I must also keep my thoughts strong. I must rediscover that being gay is magical. I must remake my world. I must work toward happiness.

He took a piece of chocolate from the drawer of the nightstand by his bed. In the morning he'd gone to the grocery store. Sara had driven him there, and she came back later to pick him up. He'd wandered about the aisles of vegetables and fruits and ended up buying a bar of chocolate and a blue flower. He took them to the counter. "You must be in a romantic mood," the cashier said. Peter felt embarrassed. "I guess I must be," he answered, "I hadn't thought about it." His intent was to take the chocolate home and dissolve it in hot water as people do in French novels. He was bored, or was he on the brink of something? He felt a slight panic. He believed he might go crazy very easily right then. His head was bursting. It's all up to me, he thought. I can go out of control right now or I can remain calm. I can trust nature. My head doesn't have to burst. He tried not to count up all the deaths he'd known – Bruce's, Ken's, John's, Artie's, Yale's, his granmother's . . .

When he got home he looked out the window of his house. At night, across the lake, he could see colored Christmas lights strung up on the docks along the water. Some of them were flashing.

And tomorrow morning when I wake up I'll just be starting over again. I'll have to take my day, shape it in my hands and make it beautiful once more. This will take concentration. It will take discipline. It will take strength. Will it be easier someday?

And what will the newspapers say tomorrow? Will there be startling AIDS headlines? "In a time when ethics are seemingly being reshaped overnight . . ." began an editorial in the Arts and Entertainment section he skimmed that evening.

He tried to think of his first disillusionment. Religion. This was followed, at the age of twenty, by the election of Ronald Reagan. Most of the young liberals, Peter knew back then were fresh out of high school, and accepted this situation without dread. No one hated Reagan enough. He allowed himself moments of joy when he was certain that a revolution would take over the country in only a matter of years. No one would tolerate Reagan. But by the mid-eighties he was still shocked to see that the president was popular. Then AIDS came along and Peter was suddenly a direct victim of the government he'd hated, or at least a victim of the times.

He needed to believe that a positive philosophy and good health were inseperable. Could it be that AIDS was caused by a lack of love?

He walked up to his parent's house and found that no one was home. They must be at the store, he thought, or out Christmas shopping. He went into the indoor pool room and gazed at the water. He took off his shoes and put a foot in. That's not cold, he thought. Then an idea raced through his mind: When was the last time I allowed myself to go swimming? he wondered. He was always avoiding what one friend had called his "physical sensual life." Downstairs he searched the sauna room for one of his father's swimming suits. He couldn't find one. Impulsively, he jumped out of his clothes and ran upstairs to the pool. He dove in laughing. As he went to the bottom of the pool, getting water up his nose and not caring if it ached, he started to cry. Then he laughed again. I sound like an animal, he thought. What he felt was a special and rare euphoria.

20

It was dawn, Christmas Eve, and Peter went up to the top of the driveway to get the morning paper before his father. He flipped through the sections as he came down the walk to his parent's house. Without looking too hard he found the usual article on AIDS:

"Often just out of college, many young people have left for New York or Chicago or San Francisco, ambitious and bursting with notions about life in a glamorous metropolis. For gay men, there loomed all this and more: the promise of tolerance in the city, a chance to live openly a life that had been unspeakable back home. But their dreams have been mocked by AIDS. And they return to their small towns, not in triumph over success in the city, but instead they come home to die. They often return to Mom because her arms are usually open, even as so many doors are slamming shut...." Peter stopped before the fence and leaned against it as he read on: "When her son first came home she did not sleep for seven days. She stopped going to bingo so she could watch over him and make sure he took his prescribed pills every four hours. She now spends time clipping newspaper articles about AIDS research and experimental treatment."

This is awful, Peter thought.

Charging into his parent's bedroom, he fell down beside his mother. She smiled. Across from her was a fire burning in the fireplace. Peter's father got out of his bed, and went into the kitchen.

"Too bad you're awake," Peter said.

"Why?" his mother asked.

"Because then I could jump on the bed and wake you up."

She kissed him. "You brought me the newspaper, didn't you?"

He gave it to her. "I found the AIDS article before you did."

They both smiled.

"Merry Christmas Eve," he told her.

"Why don't you sit closer to the fire?" She said, examining him. "You're shivering."

"I'll sit next to you," he answered, taking some of the blanket from her and wrapping himself in it. "Were you able to sleep last night?" he asked.

The newspaper lay between them.

His mother stared at the fire for a long time. He couldn't tell what she was thinking.

"I have a poem for you," she said. "I came across it this morning. 'Peter and Sara's thought will remain all through the years. A happy time spent with fun, games, and love taught.' I wrote it when you were growing up."

Although it was not time yet, he went downstairs to get one of his small presents for her from underneath the Christmas tree. He discovered Sara rummaging about among the boxes.

"So, what did you get me this year?" she asked Peter in a direct manner.

Sara's attitude toward Christmas was never a surprise. As a young girl she'd looked for price tags on her presents, and when she found them she would hold them up for inspection. She was only gracious when the price was a high one. The giving and receiving of gifts was serious: if you loved Sara you bought her a wonderful and expensive gift. She made remarks about relatives who did not spend much on gifts.

Sara, he thought, expects me to give her a great present. She also thinks that by giving me one it will make up for the lack of attention from her this year. "It's not that easy," he wanted to tell her, but then he remembered that his mother had always openly spoiled her.

"Are you going to tell me or not?" she asked him again.

"You'll find out what I'm giving you tomorrow, like everyone else."

Peter's father entered the room on his way back to bed.

"And what did I get?" he asked in a playful tone. At Christmas time he was like a little child.

Peter carried his small present back toward the bedroom, meeting his mother in the hallway.

"Put it back," she said gently. "Let's open them tomorrow."

He took it back and hid it among the others and then joined her for brekfast. She's right, he thought, there's no hurry.

"Petey-boy, how do you feel? Would you like me to make you breakfast?"

She made waffles for Peter and his father, and Sara went back downstairs to bed.

While they ate silently Peter couldn't help thinking: "Christmas will never be the same again" — it was something Sara had first said. That was in 1975, and Peter's grandmother had just died. It was true, Christmases never were the same again. The feelings of happiness were only attempts to regain that earlier joy. Christmas was for children. And next year it's going to be even more different. Peter thought, when I'm not here, but they don't know about that. They'll refuse to see that as long as they can. But they'll learn to be happy again somehow; it's not the past – me, or my grandmother, either – they'll miss something else. You learn other reasons for happiness.

Later, when they'd finished eating, his mother kissed Peter on the cheek. "You feel hot," she said. "Are you okay?"

"I'm okay," he said hurrying off. He had to go down and wrap more presents. He was giving his mother a teaball and a fake diamond ring. For his father, there was a jigsaw puzzle, and for Sara, he'd gotten tickets for free time at the tennis court.

When he came back up to the house, they'd all disappeared into their rooms for more gift-wrapping projects. Peter put a kettle of milk and chocolate to warm on the stove. Then he left, to stack the last of his presents under the Douglas fir.

"You'd better watch your hot chocolate," his father called from the kitchen. "It will boil."

So turn it down if it does, Peter thought, irritated. He looked at the yellow, blue, red, and green lights mixed in with the boughs of the tree. He remembered each of the ornaments from earlier years. One of them had his name on it.

If he were a ghost, Peter thought, he would like to float through the neighborhood and peer into all of the windows of the houses. Then he would go by his own house and see the Christmas tree in his parent's living room. He would see everyone wrapping up presents in separate rooms, and he would have to think: Now, here is a happy family.

He'd helped his father cut down the tree a week before. They were out in the mud and it amused Peter to notice that neither he nor his father was stronger than the other. It wore them both out to saw at the thick stump. When they decorated it, Peter and his mother had taken all the ornaments in boxes down from the attic. "House paint, brushes," were the words written on some of the boxes in his grandmother's handwriting.

Peter had put up as many decorations as he could. The branches were heavy with them, and his mother let him do exactly what he wanted. In the past her trees often had color themes; this year, she said, it would be potpourri.

"You do one side of the tree and I'll do the other," Peter had said, trying to decide what he might do to make the tree look silly.

Together they worked steadily at hanging all the curious objects.

"Didn't you kids help your grandmother make some of these?" She held up several regal gold and orange balls.

"We made them the Christmas before she died," he answered.

"Why aren't there any big red balls anymore?" she asked.

"The dogs used to break them off with their tails when they got too close to the tree," he told her.

He dug to the bottom of the boxes, using up even the very smallest balls — those that looked like tiny tomatoes. He took the Nativity Scene out.

"Line them up nicely," his mother instructed.

He felt inclined to line the figures up on opposing sides as he'd done when he was a kid, when the baby Jesus in the middle and all the people gathered around to fight for him, like relatives in a marriage settlement.

Peter's favorite ornaments had been the hand-carved German carolers with black robes and round hats. Their mouths were shaped in pink circles, and one of the dolls' heads could be removed. The trees that went with the flat carved buildings were made so that the curls resembled branches.

But what had happened to the fluffy gossamer angel with the silver halo? She used to perch on the rough brick fireplace, the same fireplace against which Sara had pushed him as a child so hard that the socket of one of his eyes filled with blood. He remembered afterward being taken by his mother in an open-topped MG to the hospital.

He remembered that his mother used to keep lists of the gifts each of her children received during what Peter's father's German mother called "that lovely ceremony." These lists were made so that Peter and Sara knew whom to thank later. I wonder if Mom will keep her usual lists?

They now sat by the fire in the living room listening to Rachmaninoff; his mother read Kawabata and Peter, *Food Is Your Best Medicine.* He was reading outloud intermittantly: "In almost all cases the use of drugs in treating patients is harmful. Drugs often cause serious side effects, and sometimes even create new diseases. The dubious benefits they afford the patient are at best temporary. . . Far too many of these new 'miracle' drugs are introduced with fanfare and then revealed as lethal in character, to be silently discarded for newer and more powerful drugs which cure all the ills to which the flesh is heir." A friend from California had sent him the book for Christmas. Then there was the *AIDS Treatment News Bulletin* he'd received the other day. He read aloud: "Recent studies in San Francisco and New York have found major, unexpected improvement in median survival after an AIDS diagnosis, and in long-term survival. And many physicians with large AIDS caseloads are having far fewer deaths in 1987 than in 1986, and fewer complications serious enough to require hospitalization, even though they have more patients."

After awhile Peter's mother looked up from her book and stared at him for some time. It seemed to Peter as if she were spellbound, in a coma, her eyes open.

"What's wrong?" he asked.

"Nothing," she said, continuing to stare. "I just didn't sleep last night. I'm getting tired."

Peter put down his book and looked at the fire. His father had turned on the TV to watch high school football. Gradually he increased the volume, so that it began to annoy Peter, who had a difficult enough time concentrating on his reading. He felt oddly sick: his head pounded, his body ached more than usual. The voice of the sportscaster and the noise of the cheering crowd put his nerves on edge.

While he listened to the game Peter's father took a toy train set from the closet. "He's just like a kid with toy trains and kites," Peter's mother pointed out. He watched as his father put up the track around the presents at the base of the tree. The train circled around noisily. My father *is* just like a kid, he thought. And I'm the grown-up; I'm the father sitting here reading a book.

"Where's Sara now?" his father asked.

"She's downstairs," Peter's mother answered, still staring. "Maybe she's with her boyfriend. Or she's in the sauna. Who knows?"

"She'll come up when we open the presents tomorrow," Peter said sarcastically. He knew they wouldn't see her at dinner. She didn't like her mother's cooking: the usual excuse.

He wondered what decision his mother would make a year from now when hanging up the Christmas stockings. There they were now, tacked to the fireplace with Sara and Peter's names, their mother and father's. Next year would his mother bring herself to hang all of them? Or would she be forced to pack his stockings away with the other broken ornaments for that one Christmas that would never come?

"Maybe I should take a nap," his mother said.

"I'll join you," his father announced.

"I don't want you to follow me around," she told him.

Peter was stunned. He knew this had hurt his father's pride, that he'd hide in some corner and sulk and try to make everyone feel guilty.

"He's so strange," his mother muttered.

When Peter was alone, with the firewood his father had piled up the day before, he helped himself to several of the pieces in order to keep the fire going. When his father passed through the room again, hearing the sparking of the fire, he seemed angry. I'm using the wood that he cut up for his wife, Peter thought, to make her happy; he didn't cut it up for my enjoyment. If Peter's father wanted to argue, Peter would indicate that the firewood itself came from the last of his grandmother's real estate business signs. If it came right down to it, he knew his grandmother would have preferred Peter to enjoy whatever warmth the kindling could provide. But Peter's father said nothing. He simply made a great deal of noise, storming up and down the living room.

Peter, who was still cold, lay on the couch wrapped in a blanket. Yes, he is just like a little child, he thought. Like a dream he remembered her saying. . . .

"Why don't you go down to bed?" His mother was standing there, looking down at him. He had been dozing. "I think it's inconvenient for everyone if you sleep here."

"It's cold down at my house," Peter argued lightly. "I'll have to get a base heater."

"Turn up the vents," she suggested. "Base heaters are dangerous."

"I did turn up the vents," he said.

"Then dress more warmly."

He took his blankets and went outside and down to the caretaker's cottage. Mom is just tired, he thought. I should try to make it easier on her. I must remember this when I see everyone at dinner.

Making his way down the trail he thought: Feelings aren't familiar anymore. I wish I could feel something familiar. I don't want another dimension. I'm a coward; I just want my old self back, however, shameful, wrong, or absurd. I can't take much more. But I will, I have to. I must go on, for my mother's sake. But, no, I don't want my old self back. I want something better.

It was Christmas Eve. He knew he was supposed to be feeling it. But he was not. He didn't know what to feel. When he was a kid it seemed as if things happened; now it seemed as if he had to make them happen. Christmas Eve. Saying it didn't cause any reaction. He took a tranquilizer and decided to throw out every article of black clothing he owned. He put his jackets, sweaters, pants, and shirts into bags to give away. After doing that he was able to sleep.

At midnight the entire family attended Christmas mass. Peter stared up at the pipes of the organ that jutted up like a steel mountain range behind the pulpit. As a child the entire altar reminded him of the room where the Wizard of Oz lived. There were white lanterns hanging from the ceiling with little black crosses on them. It was dark. Peter had to rely on memory to see the figures in the stained glass windows. He could hear the choir singing:

"Ah, now in sleep, as stillness enfolds him, the pain will stop. Cold and storm blow around him. With what shall I clothe him? What can I give the child? O, all you angels, keeping watch over us, quiet the branches, my child is asleep."

When the Eucharist was over, the congregation went out onto the lawn of the church carrying candles. He could almost imagine that it was not his mother but his grandmother standing next to him, with her Mona Lisa smile, her white gloved hands holding the Common Prayer. He laid his head on her shoulder.

"Did you know Aunt Neoma?" he asked, holding his candle in the dark.

"She died before I was born," his mother answered.

"Was Aunt Neoma really so unhappy?" Peter said.

"Life wasn't what she'd hoped it would be," his mother answered. "That's all I know. She was talented and she died of TB." She cupped her hand so that her candle would not go out.

People had begun to disperse, heading for the parking lot.

"I've also felt betrayed by people," Peter said.

"I don't understand," his mother said.

"Nobody understands." Peter put his finger into the hot wax of his candle. He thought of the poem his mother had read to him that morning, from the time when he was growing up. "Love taught," it had said. "But we couldn't share comfort," he now mumbled. "There was no sharing — anywhere."

"Peter," she said, "you're not being clear. Are you very tired?"

They could hear the wind in the tree tops.

"What are you thinking about now?" he asked.

"I'm praying," she said, concentrating with her eyes now shut. "I'm praying for a cure."

"A cure for what?"

"A cure for AIDS," she said.

He could see her moist eyelashes trembling.

"But Mom," he told her. "Look at all of the candle lights."

"They are pretty," she said. But her eyes remained closed.

Peter was left alone to look at their beauty, and then he heard the familiar sound of his father's horn as the car came up the drive toward them. He could see the impatient faces of Sara and his father in the clouded window of the blue Cadillac.

Joel Redon was born in 1961 in Oregon. He studied writing at
New York University and with Paul Bowles at the American School
of Tangier in Morocco. He writes for the New York Native.
Bloodstream is his first novel. Mr. Redon was diagnosed with AIDS
in 1986. He lives in Manhattan.